# THE LAKE

## KEV CARTER

www.fancyacoffee.wix.com/kev-carter-books

# CHAPTER ONE

The early morning mist rolled off the surface of the water like it had done for countless years; the water is still and silent. Nothing lives in the lake anymore; nothing thrives there or swims in it. The water just sits there holding its secrets and waiting patiently. The rain comes and ripples the surface and the wind might blow the water about, but apart from the elements nothing disturbs the lake. No animals want to live here, no insects want to skim the surface and no fish have occupied the water for years. The lake is dormant yet it still holds the secrets that it had captured, that can never be erased but still dead to all who look over it. Strangely the water is not stagnant, not pungent with the smell that comes with stale water, the place never dries up in hot summers and it never gets too full or flooded in bad rain. Winter has never seen the lake freeze. It just stays the same, never changes and is left alone to wait out its days and nights. Sat there like a sleeping giant just resting and slumbered in its vast hole. Not too far away on the edge is an old house, it was a large built place but now is smaller than it originally was. The damage was not repaired; it was half demolished and made into a smaller house many years before. A red brick building with a large chimney stack to one end, this reached high up above the slated roof and looks out over the landscape beyond. The windows are all wooden framed and some are showing signs of rot.

The paint is gone and the bare wood has been open to the elements, it won't be long until they fall to bits or will need replacing. The exterior is better now as the ivy that was covering it got stripped back and died away some years ago. The house can now breathe. The front door has the original solid, thick oak wooden door and the frame in which it sits is still solid and strong. All in all, the place is in pretty good shape considering its age and the way it was left unattended for many years. The partial demolishment took place and it was renovated somewhat but still left empty after that too. Some years later, new life was being pumped back into it as the gas and electricity was reconnected. The water supply fixed and up and working again.

The secrets it kept and the torture it had seen would never come to light, not now, not after so long. No one wanted to live here and no one did for the longest time. When it was occupied again, no one came to see, no one wanted to come. Left to rot away and be forgotten but some things can never be forgotten. Some things are burned and branded in the mind forever and nothing or no one will ever get rid of them for you. The best you can hope for is trying to control them yourself, prevent them from rising up and snapping your head off, from pulling your heart out of your rib cage. It is a constant struggle and fight. A lot of people do it and a lot of people fail at it, suffering alone and the world not understanding or knowing the agony and torture they are in.

The place seemed to die that night, the lake stood still in time and the fire almost engulfed the whole building. Was it a miracle or a curse? Whichever way you looked at it, the whole house was not destroyed and razed to the ground. Never again was that area of the earth the same, it died and nothing ever came back to it. Arid and dry, lifeless and plain, it just existed and that is how it stayed and will stay. A dead part of the world no one or nothing wants anything to do with, the place you stayed away from and never spoke of. Nearby villages forgot about it, people never spoke of it, no one ever visited it. So the whole set up married itself to itself, the lake, the house, the surrounding area. All part of the same whole and all connected by the blackness and darkness of the rumours and fears of everyone nearby, no matter what the stories were, the urban legends, the superstitions, it all didn't change the fact the place had something wrong with it. The lake especially, although it was lifeless it did seem to have a life, a life attached to it in the fact it never aged or never changed. The water was the same all year round, it was just very odd. The whole area was the same and one day it might be explained or one day whatever it was holding might be exposed, who knows what will happen, but for now it will stay the same, the same it has been since that night, the night of the fire.

"But you are a house fly Diana, you can't go and live anywhere else you will simply die my love" her best friend Gemma mocked her as she slumped across the chair in Diana's little one bedroom apartment.

"I used to visit my aunt all the time when I was a child before she went away and got sick. I just lost contact with her but now she wants to catch up and see me again. It is amazing, I never thought in a million years I would ever see her again" she said with a huge happy smile.

"Well, tell me how she can just ring your mobile like that, I think it is a prank, you better take me along just in case" she said smiling broadly back at her friend.

"She bought me my first mobile phone and I have had the same number all my life, you know that, my God I must have only been about ten"

"Are you going to tell your mum? It is her sister after all"

"No, I have not seen her for over a year, I don't see why I should, she never liked Aunt Rose anyways and she told me to forget her when Rose got sick. I have always thought she had something to do with her not getting in touch with me you know" She ran her hand through her short blonde hair and sat up on the settee, they had chilled out there all afternoon and she was getting hungry now.

"Well you just be bloody careful! You are driving somewhere you don't know and going to see someone you have not seen in, how long? Twenty years"

"About that yes it must be at least, I will be fine. Aww, are you worried about me?" she said in a soft and caring voice, mocking her as she did.

"Shut up, you owe me money so I don't want anything to happen to you"

"Cheeky sod, anyway I do not owe you any money" she frowned at her jokingly.

"Shut up you daft cow, I am starving what are we having to eat, this being your last night before you just up and abandon me"

"Chinese, Chinese or there is Chinese" Diana said giving her the options.

"Well the first Chinese is out, the second one maybe but let's just go for Chinese"

"Sounds good to me, you go get the wine from the fridge and I will ring it through, you want the usual I suppose" Diana said taking her mobile and ringing the local take away.

"Why I am always made to work when I come here, I am a guest for Christ sake" Gemma complained jokingly as she jumped off the chair and headed into the kitchen area to get one of the bottles of wine they got earlier out of the fridge. She popped the cork and poured two large glasses, leaving the other two bottles in the fridge. She brought the two glasses and what was left in the bottle into the main room. She placed them on the small glass coffee table in front of the chair and took her glass and sat back. Waiting for Diana to finish the ordering she then asked her,

"Honestly though, I want the address and please do keep in touch with me, I do not like to think my best mate is off by herself somewhere" she took a large drink of her wine.

"I am not a bloody child, I am quite capable of looking after myself I will have you know, be fifteen minutes by the way" Diana said reaching over and taking her drink from the table.

"What is fifteen minutes?"

"The Chinese you silly arse" she shook her head with a tut sound and took a drink of her wine. They both enjoyed the cold chill of their drinks and both smiled at each other.

"No, I know you are not a child, you just act like one, but I just want to know where you are just in case that is all, so do as you are bloody told my girl"

"Yes mummy" she said smiling and pulling a face at her.

"So when do you think you will be back, I do not mind looking after this place for you, so take as long as you like"

"Make your bloody mind up one minute you want to come with me then you don't want me to go and now you don't want me to come back?"

"Well I am just thinking it will be lovely to have a place of my own like this for a while if you know what I mean" she smiled and winked her eye then took another drink out of her glass, looking around the apartment.

"Well don't turn it into a whore house, I want it clean and tidy when I get back"

"Did you just call me a whore" she said surprised.

"Nope, that would be an insult, to a whore" she laughed and poured some more wine from the bottle into her glass and then did the same for Gemma.

"Cheeky cow you are, do you know that"

"You taught me everything I know" they both giggled and finished the bottle off and then Gemma went and got the second one. Their food arrived shortly after and they drank, ate and laughed the night away. It was early morning when they finally went to bed. They often slept together in the same bed and being best friends like they were never thought anything about it. Together since Junior School they had been friends for a lot of years and been through a lot together, the heartaches, the fun, the sadness and the tears. They never faltered with their friendship, no man or situation would ever change it as they made a pack when they were young and had always stuck to it. When Diana's boyfriend left her, it was Gemma who was there for her. When Gemma lost her job and her father in the same week a few years ago, Diana saw her through it. Nothing would ever come between them and Gemma would look after Diana's place while she was gone, she had no worries about it whatsoever.

Diana was up first and had taken a shower and done her hair before Gemma crawled out of bed. She was holding her head as she slowly walked into the room.

"Ho, look there is life after death" Diana laughed at the fragile state of her friend.

"Shut up, how come you never get a hangover, how come it doesn't affect you? Bloody cow I hate you" Gemma said sitting down on the chair slowly and softly holding her head.

"Because I am beautiful, only ugly people get hangovers and that is a fact" Diana said laughing at her friend. Who didn't even answer just sat there holding her head and quietly moaning to herself. Diana went and made herself a coffee, experience told her Gemma would not want anything and would soon be back in bed until early afternoon. Sure enough when she came back Gemma was gone and back in bed. She packed her bag and made sure she had her keys and phone with charger. She wanted to set off pretty early to avoid rush hour traffic. She sneaked into the bedroom and saw Gemma with her head under the pillow. She walked over and pushed her shoulder.

"Are you alive in there?" she asked.

"Just, are you off now?" A voice came back weakly from under the pillow.

"Well you get well soon and I will see you in a week or so" she said smiling at her friend and remembering it was always Gemma who suffered with hangovers the worst.

"Be careful, drive safely" Gemma shouted, and it hurt her head and she regretted it instantly.

"I will ring you when I get there" she left and quietly shut the bedroom door behind her. She got her bag and had a quick look around to make sure she had not forgotten anything.

Minutes later she was in her car and heading off on her way. She tried to put the address she had into her satellite navigation unit but it could not find it. She just followed the instructions she had been given by her aunt. The car was getting old and the unit probably wanted updating she thought and made a mental note to get it done when she returned. Her phone was on the seat beside her and she kept glancing at it for the directions. The day was bright and easy and she felt good. The night before had been a great laugh with her best friend and now she was on her way to see the aunt she had spent a lot of time with when she was young but just lost all contact with. It was amazing she got the text out of the blue like that; she had no idea that her aunt had kept her number. She tried to ring her but it was not answered. She texted her back and said she had a sore throat and could not talk so felt better texting. Diana never thought this strange as she was just excited to see her again. Especially since she had not spoken with her own mother for over a year, Rose was the only family she had really. Being the only child, she never really got on with her parents ever since she hit adulthood. These thoughts were all rushing through her head and the times she used to spend with Rose when she was a little girl. The wonderful things she used to tell her about when she was a girl and the things Rose and her mother used to get up to. Smiling to herself as she was thinking about it, she glanced down at the phone and followed the instructions displayed on it. Driving steady she headed up country and was soon off the motorway and heading somewhere she had never been before. Through a small village and then out to a more isolated area, very open country and then back along some small roads. She had been going for over two hours already and was worried she was lost. She slowed down and then stopped. She took her phone and looked at it, retracing her drive. She had followed the instructions her aunt had given her and she just hoped it was the correct instructions and that Rose had not made a mistake. She was in her eighties after all. It looked right as she glanced around herself and saw the old wooden windmill, yes there, in the instructions; she saw it pass the windmill on your left, keep going until turning for the village called Deighley. She felt better and set back off. She passed the old wooden, abandoned windmill and carried on. Seeing the very small sign for Deighley, she turned off for it. Heading down a single track road she had to be very careful as there was only just enough room for her car. The overgrowth on either side was very thick and it was touching her car at some points, she hoped and prayed she didn't meet anything coming from the other end. Going slow she leaned forward in her seat looking as far ahead as possible. It was winding this way and that and becoming very rough on her little car. The road surface was just a dirt track. She eventually got out onto a larger road; she glanced down at her phone again and read the directions. Straight ahead, past the cemetery, she looked right and left and couldn't see it. The place looked dead, there was no one about and the fields were empty, no animals and no livestock. It was deadly quiet and she started to feel a little uneasy. Then she saw the sign for the cemetery. It was unusually large on a wooden post by the side of the road, as if it was the most important place around and they didn't want you to miss it. Taking a deep breath she carried on and headed down the quiet deserted road. She came around the bend

12

and saw the large cemetery ahead of her sprawled out and was the largest she had ever seen. The road went up by the side of the old stone wall that surrounded it. She looked out across and could see the gravestones and how old there were, some tilted to the side and some had fallen over. She wondered how old the place was. She stopped and got out of her car, stood and looked out across the vast area from her elevated point and she could not understand why the place was so big. There seemed to be no villages or towns for miles around. It was deadly quiet as she looked around her and could see nothing and come to think of it, she had not seen one person, not a single soul. There was an open field to her right and the road straight ahead, the Cemetery took up all the left side of her view. She shivered for a moment and got back into the car, she locked the door and felt a little uneasy, it seemed unnatural to her all of a sudden.

Taking her phone she rang Gemma, it rang and rang but there was no answer, she knew why and thought she would still be sick in bed. The thought made her smile and she then carried on looking at where to go next. It said head for two miles or so on this road until you come to the old oak tree that reaches over the road. Should be easy to find she thought and headed back off and away from this dead place. Travelling easy and taking more and more notice that she is seeing nothing and no one, she kept an eye out for the tree. It was a large and old tree reaching out its branches like a giant dormant monster across the road; the solid thick trunk was rooted in the field on the other side of the crooked and buckled stone wall. It was a heavy, bulky and aged tree; the branches were thick and strong. She drove past it and under the stretched out branch above her head, looking up at them as she did. Also she looked back in her rear view mirror as she went on her way. She thought the giant was looking at her and holding out its arms across the road to protect her from something, smiling at her silly thought she carried on. Driving up a steep hill she finally saw the stretch of water ahead, this must be the lake and she sighed out knowing she must be near now. Heading across the small junction she went for the cluster of trees the directions told her to go for, then to the wooden bar gate across the drive. She drove slowly and under the trees could see the gate ahead of her, it was being held open by a young man who was staring at her intensely from the side of the road. He had one eye out of line to the other one and it made him look a little odd, especially when he was looking straight at you because one was not doing so. Dirty and unshaven he looked and was unclean, he was dressed in an old overcoat tied in the middle by string, his trousers were dirty and he was wearing boots that looked too large for him. She smiled at him and nodded, he said and did nothing as she drove through. She could see in her mirror

14

he closed the gate after her, and then walked off the other way. She thought no more about it but had to smile thinking what Gemma would be saying right now if she was with her. She headed down the dirt road seeing the house ahead and knew this was it, she had made it.

The place looked still and silent. The sounds you normally hear in the country like birds and the humming of wildlife was not present, it was deadly silent. She pulled up to the front and looked at the old, red brick building in front of her. She could see it had been bigger in the past but had a rebuild and renovation at some point to make it work as a smaller house. The windows were all wooden and looked in need of an update. She looked at the large chimney stack reaching up high and could see the smoke coming from it spots on top. The door slowly was opened and Diana got out of the car, she stretched and then saw her, the frail little old lady stood in the doorway that dwarfed her small frame, she smiled and held out her hands to greet her. Diana instantly got a lump in her throat, she looked so old and small and fragile but was smiling and holding her hands out for her to come forward.

"Diana my little angel" she said in a feeble weak voice.

Running from the car she went to her and smiled and looked this little old lady in the eye, the memories came flooding back to her and she could not help but cry as she reached out, held her and hugged carefully. There was a funky smell to her but she was very old and nothing ever bothered Diana like that, she was just so glad to be able to see and hold her again. She was dressed in old clothes and had two jumpers on, a long skirt and some old slippers; she must have been very hot Diana thought. Her hair was gray and long, tied back like she used to have it from when she remembered her from before. Although she was old, she looked remarkably well and her eyes seemed much younger and were smiling as she looked into Diana's eyes.

"Rose, I am so glad to see you again, so glad you texted me" Diana finally said wiping the tears from her eyes and pulled back to look at her Aunt up close.

"Oh you have grown into a fine, fine young woman my lovely" Rose said smiling.

"You look amazing Rose, oh my God you look so good, how have you been, where have you been, there is so much I want to ask you and tell you" she got all excited and smiled wide again wiping her eyes as she felt a tear come back.

"Oh well lets go inside and I will make you a hot chocolate, do you remember you used to love them and I made you them all the time when you were little"

"Yes, yes you did, oh I have missed you Rose" Diana said following the little lady into the house. It was dark inside and all the curtains were closed. The place felt damp and was dark, although it was tidy and clean there was just something wrong and Diana could not put her finger on it. She looked around as they walked through the small hallway and into the large living room. All the furniture was old fashioned and wooden, it had a lot of character but also could have done with some modernisation. The old thick blue velvet curtains were drawn closed across the large bay windows and the light had no chance of penetrating them at all. The room was lit by a lamp on a fancy wooden table in the corner and the light was coming from the hallway. Rose showed her into the room and pointed to the old large warm couch.

"You sit there my lovely and I will go make your drink"

"Do you want me to help, it really is no bother"

"No, I will have none of that, you have had a long drive and must be tired, sit there I will be back shortly" she smiled at her and shuffled off out of the room. Diana wanted to go and help but she got the impression she would not be welcomed so just took it as it was and went and sat on the worn fabric couch. Looking around she saw the wallpaper was decades out of date on the walls. The carpet, although very expensive, was very old and worn; it matched the rest of the room perfectly. It was like going back in time to another era, another moment long ago; she stretched and took out her phone. She could see there was no signal.

Cursing she stood up and lifted the phone up in the air and moved around the room, but still there was no signal. Going to the window she pulled the heavy curtain back and saw the dirty windows. Dead flies on the window sill had dried up and obviously been there for some time. She put her phone towards the dirty glass but still there was no signal. Coming back to the middle of the room she put the phone away and went to sit back down. Then she noticed it, there was no mirror or no pictures, no photos of any kind. The room was void of any photos or pictures at all. The walls were rather bare or had shelves on with little trinket ornaments all nondescript and dusty. She found it a little strange and looked over to the large sideboard, but again no photo frames and no pictures. Just an old cover and an empty glass bowl in the middle. It was not long before Rose came back with her hot chocolate. She shuffled slowly into the room and came up to Diana, she held out the mug of hot chocolate and smiled at her.

"There you go my dear, I hope you enjoy it" she said smiling then went and sat in the old tatty chair just across from the couch, she eased her little body down into it carefully and then sighed, looking across to Diana and smiled.

"Made with milk just like you used to like it" she said smiling at her.

"You remembered, Rose, thank you so much" she took a sip of the drink and noticed the small chip on the rimmed edge of the mug, she turned the mug around and drank from the opposite end. It was hot and tasted good, she had not had it for so long and it brought back good memories. She looked at Rose who was staring at her quietly, and she nodded and hummed in agreement at the taste of her hot chocolate. Holding it in her hand she asked,

"How long have you lived here, I had no idea, I am sorry we lost touch I do not know what happened Rose"

"Don't worry your young little self my dear, I have asked you here to give you something and hope it will be a surprise for you. When your were ten I went away but I never forgot you and never will forget you" she smiled and looked Diana directly in the eye, which she found a little off putting but smiled at her then looked away at the room.

"It is a beautiful house, how long have you lived here and please tell me what my surprise is Rose, you know what I am like when someone says that, I just can't rest until I know"

"Well it is a surprise and I will tell you very soon. I have lived here for many years now, this place holds memories for me and is a special place, there is no other place like this on the planet my dear" she grinned again and Rose took another sip of her hot chocolate.

"Do you live here alone; it must be difficult living in such a large place by yourself?"

"Being alone is the best you can be sometimes, do you remember when you were very young and we lost you, then finally found you in that cupboard, you were hiding from your mum and fell asleep, we looked everywhere for you and never could find you. It was not until you awoke and crawled out, we all jumped and you scared us to death because we were all sat there worried sick then suddenly you crawl out of the living room cupboard"

"Oh yes, I had forgot about that, my mum was furious, she had called the police and had to explain to them I had turned up but lied to where I had been" Diana laughed and shook her head at the thought of it all.

"Well at that time you were alone, and it was a good time for you, not for everyone else but for you it was a good time. Are there times now you wish you were alone?"

"I fell asleep then I think Rose, but I am doing alright, I am single but have a few good friends, I never feel alone to be honest"

"But when you are is it good, is it good to feel alone and not bothered by other people?" her voice changed slightly and Diana could detect a hint of annoyance.

"I like my own space sometimes yes" she said smiling but only so not to upset her, she was a little confused by her question and attitude towards it.

"Well I am glad to hear that, we have a lot of catching up to do and I have things to show you and then I will reveal the secret, I am sure you will like it" she had a warm smile again and looked very kind and small sat in the old chair across from her. Diana smiled back at her and took another sip of her hot chocolate.

"Who was that man who opened the gate for me, he looked a little odd?" Diana said with a smile and hoped it didn't come out wrong the way she said it.

"Travis, they call him Travis, why does he look odd to you?" she said frowning and not seeming to understand what she meant.

"Oh nothing I didn't mean anything by it, probably a very nice man"

"No, he is not, but he comes in useful from time to time, for opening gates and such"

Diana smiled and nodded, she was a little confused and felt a bit awkward, she took another sip of her drink and looked around the room again. She could feel Rose staring at her and when she returned her gaze, Rose smiled and seemed to sink back into the chair almost.

"Well, tell me what has been happening with you Rose, where have you been all these years, were you living here all this time?" Diana asked smiling through her slight concern that she was feeling and the unease that had crept into her head.

"I moved about a little then settled here yes, this place has a lot of history for me, you never knew about it but it is a special place. Tell me what you have been up to Diana?"

"Oh well nothing much, I went through school, went to college then dropped out. I had a wild couple of years but now I'm settled and happy with my life"

"When you were a young girl you wanted to be a nurse, why did you not become a nurse?"

"Oh that's right, yes I did, it is amazing you remember all these things Rose"

"I remember what I am told, what I am told I remember" she smiled a little smile but her eyes were not smiling she was again staring at Diana's eyes.

Taking her phone from her pocket Diana looked at it, there was still no reception or signal, she sighed and put it back in her pocket explaining,

"I was supposed to give my friend a ring when I got here but there is no signal, do you have a phone I can use Rose?"

"I do not have such things, I am sorry; maybe you will get through later. Do I make you nervous dear, you seem on edge, I am not going to bite I am just your Aunt Rose?"

"No, no sorry, not at all, she laughed out nervously in case she had offended her, I know you are my Aunt Rose, so come on lets catch up, how about if I take you out for a meal tonight, there must be a local pub or restaurant somewhere?" Diana smiled at her.

"I am afraid there is no such establishments dear, I got us some food in if you are hungry, would you like me to make you a sandwich?" she started to painfully rise out of the chair.

"No, Rose you stay there I am fine, we can eat a little later, I am sorry, I tell you this hot chocolate is lovely, I will have to start getting it again myself" she took another drink of it and smiled gratefully at Rose.

"You always liked it, I remember. You might find this place a little strange to begin with but you will get used to it, I hope we can have a good time together, I have missed my little Diana"

"I have missed you too Rose, have you spoke with mum recently, she is not talking to me again, I have not spoke to her for over a year?" She finished her hot chocolate in one last drink and put the mug on the floor beside her. She leaned forward and rested her elbows on her knees and put her hand out in front of her, interlocking her fingers together.

"Mum? No I have not spoken to her, why does she not speak to you?"

"We had another fall out, yet again, just too demanding and controlling you know?"

"Yes I can imagine, do you remember when you were young you used to dress up in your mum's high heel shoes and walk around the house thinking you were all grown up?" Rose spoke and looked at Diana but she seemed emotionless when she did, it was only after she caught herself that she showed any kind of emotion in her face. Diana had noticed it but she said nothing.

"That's right I did, so tell me Rose how do you get on here all by yourself, it is a big house to look after?" she asked again knowing she didn't get an answer the first time.

"Memories, and a long time I have been here, I have help from a local handy man, the odd man who opened the gate for you, does some jobs around here for me from time to time" she answered plainly.

"Oh I see, it really is a great place I must say, very isolated, and there is a lake I noticed"

"Yes there is a lake, but do not go near it, very dangerous place my dear" she smiled at her and shifted in her chair.

"Is there anything I can do for you Rose while I am here, is there anything you need?"

24

"Oh I will think of something no doubt" she grinned and started to laugh out loud at her and pointed out her finger at her as she did.

"Oh I am sure, you were always a shrewd one Rose" Diana laughed back seeing Rose found it all very amusing for some reason.

"Let me show you to your room Diana you seem on edge, you might want to lay down or freshen up, I have running water here" she eased slowly up out of the chair and Diana got up to help her. They walked to the front door and Diana noticed the excessive amount of indoor locks on it, bolts and chains and deadlocks. She was going to make a joke about it but stopped herself. She went to her car and got her bag out then made sure the car was locked and came back in. Rose closed the door and proceeded to lock all the locks and bolt all the bolts. She then led the way up the wooden stairs. They were bare and creaked when they stood on them making their way up, the banister was old and loose in places so Diana didn't touch it. The upstairs was pretty much like the living room, old and worn with no pictures anywhere, the carpet was worn down to the floor boards underneath. Rose stopped at the first room on her left, she opened the door and smiled as she went in and Diana followed her in. Yawning, Diana felt tired all of a sudden; she put her hand over her mouth and then put her bag on the single bed in the centre of the room.

"This is your room, the bathroom is on the left down the way there, please, feel free to make the place your own while you are here my dear" Rose said then smiled and left the room rather quickly before Diana could say anything. Diana said thank you but was not sure if she heard her as the door was closed. She felt bad for a moment and hoped she had not offended her Aunt in anyway. She went over to the window and opened the closed curtain. It was on a wooden curtain pole and the wooden eye hooks scraped across it making a sticking sound. It obviously had not been pulled open for a very long time. She saw how dirty the windows were and tried to open one. It was a wooden frame, she pulled the latch up and pushed but it would not move. She hit the frame with her hand but it was solid shut and staying that way.

Looking out of the window where she could in gaps of the dirt, she could see the lake; it was not too far away and looked dead. She peered out towards it and then around the place, just bare and desolate surroundings. Sighing she turned around and looked around the place. The faded wallpaper was older than she was, the bed looked like it was going to collapse any minute and the old fashioned wardrobe only had one door on it, the other was missing completely. Again there were no pictures or a mirror in the room and it was damp and cold. She had planned on staying for about a week but she made the decision there and then to not stay more than a few days.

Just then her phone buzzed in her pocket, she quickly took it out to see there were two bars on it, she had a signal. She quickly answered it with great relief.

"Hey, Gemma how you feeling?" she said in a low voice.

"I have been ringing and ringing you girl what is happening?" Gemma's voice came back.

Her phone then buzzed with missed call notifications, as she had just got signal.

"I had no signal, are you feeling alright, and how is your headache?" she said softly.

"Are you there, are you alright why are you whispering?" Gemma asked concerned.

"Yes I am here, it took some finding, all is good I am just being quiet, it is a very quiet place, old and falling to bits but quiet, you would hate it" she giggled and looked at the door to make sure she was alone.

"What do you mean, are you ok Diana" Gemma's worry grew in her voice.

"Yes I am fine don't worry, it is just not what I expected, I will probably be coming home early to be honest, she is looking very old but acting a little strange, just probably old age and feeling the same about me, we will be fine, don't worry" Diana reassured her friend.

"Well you keep in touch and bloody send me your location you never left it you daft cow, be careful Diana. Do you want me to come up?"

"I will be fine, it is just isolated, I didn't get a signal when I got here, but now I am up in the bedroom, higher up I suppose, no phone here you see so couldn't call you, sorry buddy"

"She texted you, you said she sent you a text she must have a phone?" Gemma pointed out. Diana was smiling but then slowly stopped as she thought about it, Gemma was right but Rose said she had no phone.

"She is very old Gem, don't worry I am fine, you just look after my place for when I get back. You looked like death this morning, how are you feeling?" Diana yawned again holding her free hand over her mouth as she did.

"I still feel a bit rough to be honest; I was worried sick about you, why don't you go get a Hotel or Bed and Breakfast, somewhere with some comfort, you can still go visit your aunt"

"I can't do that, it will offend and insult her; she has tried so hard here, I will be fine"

"Well you keep in touch I do not like you out there in the middle of nowhere with Norman Bates' mum, be careful, promise me" Gemma insisted.

"Hey stop being disrespectful and yes I will keep in touch. I know where I can get a signal now, here in my room, all is good" Diana said as convincingly as she could.

"Send me your location"

"I will I am just going to have a nap, I am knackered" Diana said yawning again.

"It is all that booze last night catching up with you"

"Probably, chat soon Gem, thanks for caring"

"Anytime and every time buddy, bye"

"Bye" she held the phone down in her hand and laid out on the bed, she felt tired and weak. Putting her phone on the little bedside table she laid back looking up at the water stain on the dirty ceiling above her head. She felt drained and tired, weak and sleepy. She closed her eyes and fell into an instant sleep. It was only minutes later her door slowly opened and Rose walked in and over to her. Looking down at her sleeping, she just stood there staring at her for a few minutes then gently reached out and touched her forehead. Running her fingers back through her short blond hair, she tilted her head and brought her hand down over her face and down across her body. She stopped and lifted her fist and held it above her face, holding it there she looked at her clenching her fist so tight it made her hand shake and then slowly brought her hand back and backed off herself. She went over and closed the curtains. Looking around she seemed to be remembering something and looking at Diana asleep on the bed she came back to her side. Just staring at her but not having any expression at all. She reached out and touched her again, feeling how young and soft her skin was. Diana had no idea she was there and no idea what was going to happen while she was here, she was sound asleep and Rose watched her for the longest time before leaving again, closing the door behind her.

# CHAPTER TWO

Gemma was worried after she had spoken to her best friend. She had known her all her life and knew when something was wrong, something was bothering her. Diana was worried about something, and not telling her what, she could just sense it. She went and got a shower and took some more tablets, her head was feeling better but she still had a nagging pain. After her shower she made herself some food and then waited for Diana to ring or text her again. The night came and it was getting late, Gemma texted her friend and could see it had been delivered but not read, she texted her another two times before ringing her. The phone rang but there was no answer. She was about to try it again when her phone rang, she looked and saw it was Diana.

"Hey are you alright what happened, I have been texting you?" Gemma said glad she had rang her back finally.

"Yeah, I just knocked out hard, was so tired, Sorry, I don't know why I am so bloody tired"

Her friend's voice sounded confused and half awake.

"Diana what the hell, come on girl wake up, are you sure you are alright, you are worrying me here, this is not you" Gemma said highly concerned.

"Gemma I am fine, just tired, please do not worry, I will be fine, I am getting up now and will be in touch stop worrying" she pressed the phone off and flopped back down on the bed, she felt drained and tired. It was dark and the only light was coming under the door from the landing light. She managed to lift herself off the bed and go to the curtains and opened them.

She could make out the full moon in the sky and it filled the room with a bit more dim light. She then just realised she had opened these curtains before. Turning around she went and turned the light switch on, but nothing happened it was not working. She went to the door and opened it, squinting her eyes as she walked out onto the landing and looking up at two main lights from the ceiling. It was just light bulbs shining bright hanging down with no shades on. She listened but it was silent. She looked across the landing and then back towards the stairs. Slowly she started to walk towards them; looking at her little wrist watch she saw it was 2.30am. Slowly heading down the stairs and trying not to make them creak as she did, she could hear someone talking in the main room. She tried to listen but it was a low voice. She stood by the door and the voice stopped. She slowly opened the door and went in; the room was lit up with bare bulbs hanging from the ceiling like the landing. Sat in the chair was Rose she was looking over at her and smiling as she came into the room.

"You have a nice nap dear, you were very tried" she said kindly and with a smile.

"Rose, you are still up its very late, I am sorry I just knocked out, I don't know what was wrong, I am sorry I didn't mean to be so rude" Diana said rubbing her eyes.

"Not at all my dear, you had a tiring day, would you like me to make you some hot chocolate, with milk like you used to like it"

"No, its fine thank you" she came over and sat on the old couch and looked at Rose who was looking at her and smiling.

"Would you like something to eat?" Rose asked her.

"I have gone past my hunger threshold I think, but thank you anyway, you are up very late I hope you were not waiting for me?" Diana said worried she had caused her a problem.

"Not at all my dear I do not need much sleep, I am fine never worry about me"

"I thought I heard you talking to someone?" Diana said while looking around the room.

"Do you remember that imaginary friend you used to have when you were young that your stupid mother used to go crazy about it?" she smiled and showed her teeth which were bad.

"My mum used to be mad about everything I did, she still does to be honest" Diana came and sat down on the couch looking at this little old lady. She remembered her from when she was very young, but now she just seemed an old lady she was making conversion with. The magic didn't seem to be there like it was when she was young.

"Your mum is a strange one I believe" she said like she was asking a question.

"Well she is your sister, you tell me" Diana laughed and saw the lost look in her eyes for a moment then she smiled again at her and laughed.

"You never married Rose, never had children?"

"I had a boy, but he is no longer with us, it was a terrible accident, makes me sad to think about it actually"

"Oh am so very sorry I had no way of knowing, please forgive me" Diana said genuinely concerned she had hurt her feelings or bought back a bad memory.

"It is alright, so why have you not had children yet, would you not like to bring life into this world, bring the joy of creation into your life?"

"Just never happened, not met the right man Rose, I am doing alright single"

"You never want children? That just is not natural for a woman Diana" she frowned at her, with a look of distaste.

"Well it doesn't suit or fit with everyone Rose does it"

"Well it should, bringing life into this world is the most important and wondrous thing a woman can do, never forget that

34

and don't leave it until you are barren, you will regret it then and become an old nasty poisonous hag"

"Well ok Rose," Diana said holding her hands up and smiling thinking she was joking. But the nasty look she was receiving from Rose told her differently.

"I think I will go to bed now, I am feeling a little tired, hope you sleep well and do not go out of the house, there are wild animals out there and some dangers we dare not speak of" she got up and walked out of the room without looking at her or saying anything else. Diana watched her go and said no more. A little shocked Diana looked at the door for a few moments then shook her head and gasped out. Taking another look around the room she yawned and thought she might as well go to bed as well. She gave it a few minutes then walked out and quietly upstairs; she got her toiletry bag from her room and walked down to the bathroom. She carefully opened the door and searched for the light switch. It was an old fashioned brass one and she flipped the small switch. Again a bare bulb from the hanging light lit the room. It consisted of an old bath and a sink and a more up to date toilet that looked like it had been put in many years later. It just did not match the rest of the bathroom. She went and brushed her teeth and looked around for a mirror but there was none. Quickly finishing up she went back to her room. Looking out of the window, she rubbed the glass with her fingers to make it clearer so she could see through, the dirt came off and she peered out. It was pitch black except for the moonlight. A beautiful clear night and the stars were visible. She smiled at the sight and looked over to the moon. It was shining bright and big in the sky and she was memorised by it for a few moments, then looking away she thought she caught sight of some movement below her window. She glared and could not see anything, but then she was distracted by a small light over the lake. It looked like a signal, a torch maybe, but over the water or in it maybe.

As soon as it appeared it was gone and she couldn't see it again, she strained her eyes to look but could not see it again. She searched all over where she could see from the moonlight but she saw nothing else. Trick of the light maybe she thought. Pulling the curtains shut she turned around and jumped back startled. In the doorway was stood Rose smiling at her.

"Fuck, what the hell, Rose you frightened me stood there" she said gasping her breath.

Rose just smiled and backed out of the room closing the door behind her, Diana suddenly became scared and aware of the strangeness. She walked to the door and put her ear to it, listening she could hear nothing. Looking around the room she searched for a chair or something she could put up against the door handle. But she sighed out disheartened she could not find anything. She left the light on and went to lie on the bed. She didn't get in it just stayed on top. She looked over at her phone and noticed the battery was almost gone. Looking in her bag she found her charger and looked around for a plug to connect it. She could not find one at first but then found the only socket in the room. It was an old brass type and over by the door. She plugged her phone in and made sure it was charging ok. Then went to lie back on the bed, she was a bit tired but decided to stay up this night and not go back to sleep. She thought about when she was younger and what she remembered about her Aunt Rose. Going around to her house that was always neat and tidy and immaculate, the way she would never swear or get cross, always dressed nicely and respectable. When she used to come and visit she always brought some sweets for her, even when her mum complained, Rose brought them still and gave them to Diana in secret, only the two would know. Remembering how much fun they used to have together made Diana smile the way Rose always seemed happy and playful and wanting to please. Then her expression changed and she thought about today, how she seemed to have changed, it had been over twenty years but still, she seems to have changed in many ways.

Left with her thoughts Diana did not go back to sleep. As soon as the sun came up and light came flooding in through the cracks in the curtain, she quietly got up and went to the bathroom. Then she crept downstairs and unlocked the front door as quietly as she could. She went out and took a deep breath of the lovely fresh morning air. Smiling at the freshness and being out of the stuffy house, she walked off and down towards the lake. It was still early and the birds should have been singing but there were none. She looked around and across the landscape and she could not see a single bird, no animal and no wildlife at all. Finding it a little odd she carried on down the path and looked ahead. There was a fallen tree and old gentleman sat on it, his back towards her, he was looking out across the lake, his right hand resting on an old homemade walking stick. Looking back and thinking about not disturbing him she stopped, but before she could go the other way he spoke to her.

"I am not the one who will hurt you, there is no need to run away" his voice was powerful and strong. He turned his head and looked at her as she just stood there not knowing what to do at first.

"Good morning, I didn't mean to disturb you" she said to him.

"You are not disturbing me, there is nothing to disturb around here" he looked back across the lake and she walked up to him and stood next to him looking out across the lake too.

"It is very early I didn't think there would be anyone around, I am just out for a stroll" she said as an explanation she felt she had to give for some reason.

"You, staying at the house with that woman" he said not looking at her.

"Rose, yes, she is my Aunt" looking down at him she could tell he was old and had a hard life. He had one of those lived in faces, there was some scaring that had faded with age. His eyes were sagging and he was expressionless. But she didn't find him threatening and didn't feel in any danger.

"How long are you staying" he said still not looking at her.

"Not sure yet, won't be too long I imagine I have to get going, I have not seen her in twenty years, it was out of the blue I visited really"

He slowly turned and looked her in the eye then moved his eyes over her face and down her body and back. He took a deep breath and nodded out to the lake.

"This lake used to be alive, popular, full of fish, a very active spot, there used to be fishing pegs all along the banks, people came from miles around to fish here. It is dead now, and it killed everything around it"

"What happened, why is it so still and stagnant now"

"It's not stagnant it is dead, it has death in it, people stop coming because it is dead, the body is in there, you must not stay here long. You must go when you get the chance"

"Body, what, oh my god" Diana was genuinely shocked and wondered why Rose did not tell her of this, she looked back at the old man.

"They say she still walks these parts and you can see her at night. Legends grow and rumours keep people away. Nothing lives around here now; it is all dead, just like this lake"

"Oh my God, what happened did she drown was she swimming in the lake?"

"She was only young, very young, still there, still down there, you must leave and leave now, it is dangerous here for you, but you must leave, please just go away" The old man never looked at Diana as he spoke he just kept looking out to the lake. She swallowed and felt rather disturbed at this story. She shook her head and could not believe it; she looked out across the lake and suddenly became cold, a shiver went down her spine.

"That is terrible, who was she, did she live local, did they find out what happened"

The old man just slowly shook his head; he looked at her and turned to face her, his hand still on the walking stick he said in a solemn and tired voice.

"Leave, you must go now, just go back where you came from and never come back to this dead place, nothing good ever happens here"

"Why do you say such things, I am just visiting my Aunt in the house back there" Diana said not really knowing what to say because she was somewhat shocked herself.

"They should have let the whole lot burn all those years ago, but half the house was saved and the evil is still in there, the baby can never be brought back"

"You are talking nonsense now, who are you and why are you saying these stupid things?" Diana backed off and suddenly became worried and cautious. Her first initial feeling was gone and now she felt threatened and a bit uneasy.

"Leave little blonde lady, leave before it is too late" his eyes pleaded with her and he leaned forward towards her, she backed off and stepped away from him. She shook her head and backed away and left him sitting there staring at her as she went back, she hurried off and only looked back once to see him then again looking out across the lake. Walking fast she headed back to the house, she spotted the odd looking man she saw at the gate when she arrived stood by her car and looking in through the window. She walked faster and shouted to him as she approached, but at first he didn't hear her or just ignored her. She quickened her pace and was much closer when she said again.

"Can I help you, please step away from the car thank you" he looked around quickly and stepped back, he had a small wooden sign in his hands and put this behind his back as Diana got close to him. She looked at him then at her car to see if there was any damage.

"I was only looking miss, just looking that is all" his voice was as weird as his features and odd looking eyes seemed to be more childlike and much too young for the age he looked. Diana suddenly then felt a little bad wondering if he was a little retarded, she smiled and could see nothing had been done to her car as far as she could see.

"Yes its ok, I was just wondering who you are that is all, do you live around here?"

"Yes, yes I do miss, just over that way about an hour or so if I walk fast but more if I walk slow," he nodded and stood there like he was being told off by his school teacher. She looked at him and could see he was in his late twenties but acted much younger. His eyes were his most prominent feature albeit for the wrong reason. His clothes hung from him and he looked dirty and in need of a good bath. Unshaven but his hair was short and looked like it had been cut with a pair of blunt scissors by someone who didn't care what sort of job they did, she could smell his bad body odour. He started to back up and edge away but kept looking at Diana as he did, not taking his odd eyes off her.

"What do you want, why are you here so early in the morning, do you want to see Rose for something?" He looked confused at her and shook his head, looking to his side he kept going and when he was twenty feet or so he turned and ran off back up the way he had come and off towards the gate. Diana called after him but he didn't turn around. She double checked her car and could see no damage, she checked her doors and then looked out towards where he had ran; she could just see him disappearing over the hill.

He was running fast and laughing to himself, giggling uncontrollably, he then threw the small sign he had in his hand away into the side bushes. It was the wooden Deighley sign that Diana had followed the day before.

"I like her, she is going to be juicy, I, like her" he started to laugh and say to himself.

Diana walked back into the house, she was confused and had some questions she wanted answering. It had been a very strange morning. She walked in and searched around downstairs. The whole place was old and dirty and just rotting away, this is not what Rose used to be like; she was very house proud, very clean and tidy. The kitchen was about the best place she had seen so far. It was not too bad but still very outdated. There was a wooden table in the centre with two chairs only although it was big enough for four at least. She was feeling hungry and looked in the cupboards but they were all bare. All she found was a new box of hot chocolate, some bread and margarine and few tea bags. There was no fridge but a pantry she opened the door and noticed some milk and some cold meat wrapped in a plastic bag, one loaf of bread and a packet of biscuits. The oven was very old and only had two hobs with a small oven below. Rose was nowhere to be found, thinking she was still in bed Diana went upstairs and into the bathroom. Then she walked back towards her own room. Before she got there, she heard a noise and Rose shouting to her, she quickly went in and took her phone off charge and put it in her pocket.

"Is that you Diana, Diana are you there dear" she sounded sad and lonely and Diana went back to see where she was. Shuffling down the landing she came towards her, wearing the same clothes as she had the day before. She smiled at her when she reached her.

"You are up early love, are you alright, shall we have something to drink"

"Are you alright Rose, do you need any help?"

"No dear lets go downstairs and have a drink, could you help me please dear" she said and seemed to be struggling to walk today. Diana helped her down the stairs and into the main room. She sat her down and made her comfortable in the chair.

"Thank you dear, you were always a good girl, always helpful"

"I don't think there is much to drink Rose, I will go out today and get you some food and supplies you can't live with nothing in the house"

"How about some hot chocolate and I will have a tea with milk and no sugar please" Rose smiled and disregarded what she had said. She nodded her head and sat back in the chair. Diana went to the kitchen and boiled the milk in a small saucepan she found in the sink, she made them their drinks and brought them back and gave a small mug to Rose. Who smiled and was very grateful as she took it.

"Thank you dear, you are very good to your old Aunt Rose"

"Thank you Rose for having me here, could I ask you a few questions please?" Diana wanted some answers and was not happy with how this visit was going.

"Yes of course dear what are they; you know I will tell you the surprise today"

"Thank you Rose, it is just I went for a walk today by the lakeside, I know you told me to stay away but I was very careful, anyway I met a man, an old gentleman with a stick" she said taking a large drink of her chocolate.

"Horrid Travis, he is evil Diana, evil stay away from him, he tried to kill me once" she said in a matter of fact way as she sipped her hot tea.

"What? Kill you how, when, what do you mean" Diana was flabbergasted.

"He burnt the house down, I was still in it at the time, and it destroyed half the building but they were able to save the rest that is what we are living in now" she smiled and carried on sipping her drink unaffected by what she was saying.

"Rose, what the hell, why is he still around did he not get arrested" Diana asked unbelievably.

"He denied it but I know he did it, he walks about early mornings now looking at the lake, and then he wanders off again, I have no fear of him anymore"

"He told me about the girl drowning in the lake?" Diana said then noticed the change in Rose. She became still like a statue for a moment then looked up with just her eyes, not moving her head. But then started to move again and took another sip of her tea.

"I don't know what you mean, the only thing that died here was my child" she dropped her eyes and Diana regretted saying what she just said, she felt horrible inside.

"Oh no, I am sorry Rose, I didn't realise, please forgive my insensitivity, I am so sorry"

"You didn't know my dear; it was a long time ago now. But just stay away from that man he is evil and very dangerous, drink your chocolate before it gets cold"

"Why do you allow him onto your land, why is he still around here?" she asked doing as she was told and taking another large drink of her chocolate.

"He lives close, and never talks to me anymore we never meet that is why he goes there very early in the mornings" She looked at Diana and smiled at her gently. Diana felt so sorry for her at this moment and was mad at herself for thinking what she did the night before. Obviously Rose has been through much more then she could ever know.

"Well I apologise for opening old wounds please forgive me, how about you and me go out to town today I will get you a pantry full of shopping in, anything and everything you like"

"We have some food here dear, we can have a sandwich later, I have some meat and bread, I want to tell you something Diana and want you to promise me you will not tell anyone else"

"Yes of course, anything" Diana leaned forward and came closer to her and could see Rose was struggling to find the words.

"Well, please forgive me, I know things are not what you would like, and you are very posh these days with a car and expensive clothes" she looked at what Diana was wearing.

"These are not expensive Rose, just High Street off the rail stuff" she said finishing her drink.

"Well whatever that means I do not know, but please do not look down on me, I have had a hard life and it has been full of tragedy and hurt and I just want you to be happy my dear"

"Rose darling that is fine, do not worry about a thing, I never judge and certainly would not do that to you, I can see you are the same kind lovely woman I was when I was a child" she came over and hugged her and Rose reached up and hugged her back.

"Thank you dear I would not like you going back telling people about me"

"Don't be silly, I tell you what, how about I take you down to visit me in the not too distant future, we would have a laugh" Diana pulled back and looked into Rose's face and saw her smile and it pulled on her heartstrings. She suddenly felt so sorry for this Aunt who had made her childhood one of such fun and joy. The same woman who would have done anything for her, and now was living alone in a outdated run down house, lost her child and must be so lonely and miserable here all by herself.

"Thank you dear, you are wonderful, now please excuse me, I am going to spend a penny" she smiled and got up out of the chair and walked much better across the room, her shuffling was gone,

Diana didn't think much of it and let her go. She reached into her pocket and pulled out her phone and texted Gemma.

"It's me, are you up, all still good here, hope you are well and we need a night out when I get back so be ready. Text me when you can"

She put the phone back in her pocket and noticed it had not charged, the bar was still on one. She cursed and looked at the bottom where the charging cable went in, then turned it over but what she was looking for she was not sure of and shook her head and was annoyed with it.

She waited for Rose to come back and went to the window, opened the curtain and looked out of the dirty glass at her car.

She looked round and saw Rose shuffling back in. She was walking slow again and seemed to be in a bit of pain as well.

"You alright dear?" she said to Diana as she sat down.

"Yes, my phone didn't charge last night, do you get power cuts here, is your electric supply ok, the damn thing said it was charging but it hasn't.

"The power sometimes goes out yes, but you can try again now, it should be ok, go up and plug it in then come here and let me tell you something" Diana did what she was told and went upstairs. She plugged her phone back in and looked at it, it said charging. She went back downstairs and sat on the couch facing Rose who was waiting for her.

"Right my dear, I want to tell you your surprise, when you were young you always were kind to me, always happy and smiling and it made me feel good"

"Likewise Aunt Rose" Diana smiled at her.

"Well I could not give you much then, but now I am going to give you what I have, I want you to have it all" she grinned at her and waited for the response.

"You don't have to give me anything Rose, just being in touch with my favourite aunt is enough and all I need" she said then yawned and felt tired again.

"Well I want you to have this house, it is bought and paid for and I am giving it you"

"Rose, this is your home darling I can't accept that, this is all you have"

"I know it is, and I want to give it to you" she smiled and looked happy at what she had just said and was expecting Diana to be just as happy.

"This is your home Rose" Diana smiled and tried not to sound ungrateful, but she just didn't want the place.

"This is all I have and I am offering it to you, don't you want it?" Her face dropped all expression and she looked at Diana with a strange look of mistrust.

"It is a lovely place and I am very flattered but Rose, you live here and you stay here, how about we get..." but she was not allowed to finish her words before Rose interrupted her.

"I will be very sad and offended if you turn me down, that is what everyone does, everyone else just turns me down, down, down, down" she insisted with a louder voice.

"I am sorry Rose, please don't take it the wrong way I am truly flattered I really am" Diana insisted and tried to calm Rose down. She could see that she had begun to shake in her chair.

"No, no, no, everyone is the same; you were supposed to be different. You were different you were nice and were helpful and loved your Aunty Rose" she was shaking in the chair and hitting the chair arms with her fists. Diana came over and put her hands on her hands to stop her, and talked to her in a comforting voice.

"Calm down, you are right; I am very pleased I would love the place thank you" she said smiling at her and seeing she was having some sort of anxiety attack. Eventually Rose settled and just stared at the floor. She was silent and didn't move; Diana looked at her and lifted her hands off hers slowly. Suddenly Rose snapped out of it and was smiling again, looking up at Diana with her calm and happy face. Diana was instantly worried and knew something was wrong, this was not normal behaviour and she wanted to help but had no idea how to do so.

She looked at her for a moment and remembered what she used to be like when she was a small girl growing up, with her being an only child she always got spoilt but Rose did the most of it and always was happy to do so. Smiling back at her, Diana could see she was stable again and looked happy as if nothing had just happened. Wondering if it was dementia she kept it in mind and relaxed back looking at her aunt Rose sitting there quite happily and smiling.

# CHAPTER THREE

Gemma texted again as her last two texts had not been answered; she looked at her phone as soon as she awoke and noticed Diana's message. Sitting up in bed she was about to ring but uncannily just as she was about to the phone started to ring and it was Diana.

"Hey, where have you been I have been texting you?" Gemma said.

"Gemma, sorry I had my phone on charge upstairs and didn't hear you" Diana said sounding sleepy and tired.

"You alright you sound out of it?" Gemma asked a little concerned.

"Yeah, I am just so bloody tired and sleepy here; I have come to lay down a bit"

"What is wrong with you, it's not like you at all you are always full of life"

"I don't know, I am so tired, I will ring you when I wake up ok, I just can't keep my eyes open at the moment" she slurred her words as she was nodding off.

"Wait, hold on no, you tell me what is going on, something is wrong what is it" Gemma knew this was not like her best friend at all.

"Well I hate to say this but I think Rose needs help, she seems a little unstable, you know with her mind" Diana's voice had gone down into a whisper on the phone.

"I know it, I told you, don't have a shower for Christ sake" Gemma joked but regretted it when she heard the concern in her friend voice.

"I am serious there is something wrong with her, she wanted to give me the house, she has no food in, nothing, the place is falling to bits, I found out she had a son that died, people around here are strange and the lake outside the place is just bloody weird" she whispered.

"Give me your location come on now, I need to know where the hell you are" Gemma insisted. She heard Diana pressing buttons on her phone then she whispered back with surprise in her voice.

"It's bloody gone, it's not here, the directions she sent me, the texts are gone"

"Diana, get out of there now, something is not right, come on I am not kidding leave, do it now let me come and get you at least. Where are you, tell me" Gemma was shouting into the phone with a panic and worry in her voice and her hands shaking.

"Listen head north head for a place called Deighley, turn off there and go down towards , err, shit I can't remember, there is a very large oak tree across the road and then a massive cemetery the largest I have ever seen, head for the lake"

"Hold on, tell me again, think girl think, what is the full address?" Gemma was frantically writing it all down on the small note pad by the side of the bed.

"Old windmill, out in the middle of nowhere, Deighley, old oak tree and cemetery, the lake, old house here" Diana's voice was fading and she was falling uncontrollably to sleep.

"Diana, Diana" Gemma shouted. She heard nothing and was shaking and nervous, shouting her name she listened and heard the phone drop; she must of just fell asleep or passed out. As she carried on listening she heard footsteps then an old woman chuckling. She heard the phone being picked up and then it was turned off. She froze for a moment just looking at the phone in her hand then she scrambled out of bed and looked at the note pad. She tried to Google the town name of Deighley and couldn't find it, she tried on her phone maps app and still it would not come up. She started to panic and tried to think if she heard her right and she looked at what she had wrote down. She texted Diana and told her to ring or text her back as soon as she could.

Diana was fast asleep, knocked out with the drug in the hot chocolate. Rose was stood by the side of the bed and looked down at her laid out. She tilted her head to one side and gently touched her face, she moved her hair to one side and then back again. Stroking her face she just looked at her with a blank expression then she took the mobile phone, turned and walked briskly out of the room, there was no shuffle and no problem walking at all. She closed the door and left her there passed out on the bed. It was night time before Diana awoke and her head was thumping. She held it and tried to get rid of the pain that was like someone trying to hammer their way out of her skull. She moaned and tried to sit up but could not, her head felt so heavy she could not move it. Feeling like the worst hangover plus ten, she just laid there and held her head. Eventually after some time she managed to sit up and open her eyes fully, she was out of focus but could make out the darkened room with the help of the light coming in under the door. She tried to stand but was unstable and wobbly on her feet. She held onto the bed and stood there. Trying to clear her head but it would not get any better than it was. She took a deep breath and staggered to the door. She was weak and fell into it. Holding the handle she tried to open it but it was locked, she pulled and pushed it but it would not move it was solid. Falling back down to the floor she tried to cry out and call Rose but her voice was weak too. She just had no energy, crawling over the dirty floor she reached the side table and tried the light for the lamp but it didn't work. She then crawled and got to the window and pulled herself up with the heavy curtains and got her hand on the windowsill to help her get up. She pulled the curtains wide open, looked out and couldn't see anything so she rubbed the dirt off and peered out. It was pitch black and the clouds were obscuring the moon tonight so she got to see nothing. Shaking her head, she turned and took a deep breath then made a mad dash for the light switch. Falling over and crashing into the wall as her legs gave way she managed to flick the switch on as she fell onto the floor. The bare bulb seemed to burn her eyes and make her head throb at the front above her eyes.

Holding up her hands to shield herself from the light she waited a few moments to adjust and then looked around the room from her seated position. She could hardly keep her head up while looking but managed to crawl over to the bed again and search for her phone. She could not find it anywhere and the fear that was already there grew more intense and she started to cry. She sobbed and eventually passed out again on the floor.

When she awoke she was in bed it was light outside and her headache had eased but was still there, she felt terribly hungry and thirsty, her mouth was dry and she had to take a few attempts to be able to swallow. She took a few deep breaths and sat up, swung her legs around, dropped her head and moaned out. Looking for the time on her little wristwatch, she saw it was gone, her wrist was bare. She tried to look for it but could not find it anywhere about.

The ache was still there in her head just not as intense. She needed the bathroom and felt dirty and unclean. Heading for the door she tried it and to her surprise it opened. Pulling it wide she looked out into the landing area. It was clear so she stumbled out and headed for the bathroom.

Downstairs Rose was sat in her chair and humming to herself, she looked up when she heard Diana moving about upstairs. Smiling slightly to herself she carried on humming to herself and closed her eyes. Diana came out of the bathroom and carefully walked to the top of the stairs. She looked down them and got focused. Taking a deep breath she started to slowly and carefully head down, holding the banister for support as she did. She reached the bottom safely and went into the main room. Holding onto the door handle, she stood there swaying and looking at Rose sat in her chair. She shook her head and focused her eyes.

"Hello dear how are you feeling? You were not very well" Rose said smiling at her.

"Rose, what, what is happening, what is going on?" Diana managed to say while holding onto the door handle for support.

"Nothing dear, you are just not feeling too good, would you like some hot chocolate?"

Shaking her head Diana looked around the room then focused on the couch, she took a breath and went for it; she was unsteady but made it and flopped down on it with a thud and a sigh.

"Where is my phone, where is my mobile?" she asked Rose.

"I have no idea, have you lost it?" she said looking surprised.

"You have taken it, where is it?" Diana said trying to not open her eyes too much as it was causing her a migraine type of headache.

"Me, no I have not touched it dear" she smiled at her again as if nothing was wrong.

"What is happening, why are you doing this Rose, what is wrong with me?"

"Would you like a sandwich, or a hot chocolate?"

"No, Diana shouted and held her head as it thundered through her skull when she shouted, no I just want my phone please Rose, give me my phone"

"But I do not have your phone dear, have you lost it, I expect it will turn up"

Diana looked at Rose and could see she was in a very dangerous position, something was very wrong and she was in no condition to do anything about it. Slumping back in the couch she tried to fight the tiredness, she was thirsty and hungry and had to get food she knew this. She decided to play along even if just to get food and fluid.

"I am hungry, could I have a sandwich please and some water" she said not looking up from her hands where her head was sitting.

"Why yes of course, Rose stood up out of the chair and walked to the kitchen effortlessly and was gone for only about ten minutes. She returned with a single cold meat sandwich and a mug of hot chocolate. Diana ate the sandwich instantly feeling she was starving.

The hot chocolate was not welcomed as she wanted some water but decided to drink it while she could. She needed all the strength she could get. Rose sat back down and hummed while she watched Diana eat and drink her food and chocolate. Diana leaned back and thought it would make her feel better but it seemed to make her feel worse, she felt tired again. She could not move and Rose stood back up and went into the kitchen. Going to the open hot chocolate box she picked it up and brought it over to the other side. There were some tablets from a small bottle. She emptied five out and crushed them with the back of a small spoon. Humming while she was doing so, then she took the powered tablets and emptied them into the hot chocolate powder, stirring it in with the spoon. Then she cleaned it all away and went back into the living room. Diana was passed out on the couch which was no surprise to

Rose. There was a knock on the door then it opened and Rose waited for the room door to open. Moments later in walked Travis, his odd eyes looking towards Diana passed out on the couch. In his hand he had a bag with some milk and bread and a few other items he had brought over for Rose. He didn't have to be told to go put them into the kitchen. When he came back he sat next to Diana. He looked down at her and then smiled across to Rose who was now sitting back down in her chair.

"Not yet Travis, but don't worry you can have your fun later" Rose told him looking down at Diana as well.

"She is nice, I am sure this one will work, I know this one will work"

"Yes, I think it will work too, she seems to be just the right sort we need; now did you shift the car, did you clear the sign away like I told you to?

"Yes I sure did, I always do as I am told and you always tell me what to do" he smiled and looked back at Diana, who was oblivious to what was going on. He reached out and touched her hair then moved his dirty fingers and hand across her face, rubbing her lips, he looked lower and was going to move his hand down but Rose spoke and stopped him.

"There is a phone over in that drawer, I want you to destroy it and get rid of it completely do you understand me, do not keep it, do not turn it on, destroy it, I have already taken the sim card out" her voice seemed more powerful and confident all of a sudden.

"Yes I will do that, do you want me to take her back upstairs for you?" he said standing up.

"Yes go put her away in the room and lock the door, and no touching, there's a good boy" Rose told him and then started to hum to herself again.

Travis said no more to her, he bent down and with tremendous strength he easily picked the limp body of Diana up and walked upstairs with her. Rose watched him go and then leaned back in the chair; she interlocked her fingers and rested them on her lap. Smiling slightly she closed her eyes and leaned back gently humming to herself.

Gemma had already rung the police by this time and the best they could do was treat it as a missing person's case for now, it was too early for anything else. She was disgusted of how unhelpful there were. They promised to send someone around to see her but she was not convinced that would ever materialise. She was in a panic and kept methodically checking her phone for any new messages or calls. She texted Diana just about every time she picked up her phone, and then she went through Diana's things to see if she could find the address written down anywhere.

Tucker was worried, he was stood by the lakeside and he saw Travis moving the car, he hid down and out of sight. Then when the car had gone her took a deep breath, he was mustering up his courage and felt his hands shaking. He walked off towards the house; he had thoughts of the fire flooding back to him, seeing the house burning, remembering what was in there, feeling the intense heat as he stood there that night petrified. He tried to shake it from his head. The fear he felt that night and the fear he was feeling now never left him and he would take it to the grave with him, of that he was sure. He walked with his stick and was breathing heavily as he approached the front wooden door. He remembered the flames reaching high in the night sky, the building collapsing and the timber burning. He had not been this close to the house since that fateful night all those years ago. The painful memories causing him to falter, the shame he had, the regrets and the dread of it all was too much for him.

He reached the door and froze, he wanted to pound it down, rush in, shout and be forceful and strong. But he could not, he had the fight knocked and scared right out of him long before this, and he knew he would not get it back. He felt ashamed and weak, he knew what he must do but he just could not bring himself to do it. He bowed his head and sobbed. He turned and started to walk away then glanced to his side and saw the face of Rose staring at him, she was smiling and then giggling at him in a knowingly way. He shook his head and walked away back the way he had come. He was in tortured agony and was not strong enough to do anything about it. Humiliated and saddened he walked back not looking behind him knowing she would still be watching him. Out towards and then past the lake he went, heading down the small path and out to the small road. The further he walked, the greener the grass seemed to get, he could now hear a bird in the nearby tree and he took a deep breath because the air was fresher here. He headed off the estate and down towards his small cottage. It was about half a mile away and he could not wait until he was there and get in, locking the door behind him. He never looked back and his heart was heavy and sad, he dried the tears from his old weary face and headed down to his home. He walked slowly and his eyes were saddened and still wet from his tears. He relied on his stick when he walked and hobbled to the left with the stick for support. He reached for the door, took his key, opened the lock and went inside. Closing the door behind him he locked it with the key and also the three other bolt locks that were on the inside of the door. It was a simple old cottage and one that had been full of character and peace at one time. But that time was long gone, it was in a mess and the furniture was old and worn. Although it was tidy it was not a happy home. Nothing had been joyous here for many years. He should have moved away but he had nowhere to go and as the years passed he was just stuck here with his painful and haunting memories. He put his stick down by the cloth settee and slumped down into it. The tears dwelling in his eyes once again, a very broken and damaged man he sat there in silence and just stared at the empty fireplace. Above it was a picture of a young girl, a happy looking, smiling teenager. It was the only photo in the house and he spent hours just staring at it, moving his eyes from the fireplace up to the photo his eyes filled with tears and the daily heartache began for him. The noise of that night, the sights he saw and can never be unseen. The memories of him trying to take his own life, but he didn't even have the courage to do that. The anger towards the authorities not doing enough, never doing enough and now they just see him as a sad, old man who is a pest. He had given up trying to tell people what he knew, to convince anybody of anything. He breathed in and the tears fell uncontrollably as he cried and said sorry over and over to the photo above the fire.

# CHAPTER THREE

Diana was laid on the bed, her clothes all messed up and her jeans undone, she shook her head and tried to focus, she was weak but at least the headaches had gone. Lifting her head up off the dirty pillow she looked around the room. It was light outside; the curtains were just opened enough for her to see through. She lifted up and swung over to hang her feet off the side of the bed. Sitting there she got her bearings and shook her head, yawning she tried to wake up fully. She had, had enough of this, something was very wrong and she wanted to go home. Standing up and steadying herself she got herself balanced. Then went to the door and tried to open it, but it was locked, she pulled and then banged on the door.

"Rose, Rose why is this door locked, let me out, Rose" she shouted as loud as she could. Banging some more she kicked it, in anger. Going to the window she tore down the curtains and threw them onto the floor, the dust was knocked out of them, and dispersed everywhere making her cough, the wooden rings dancing on the pole where they were left and the curtain torn off. Looking out of the window she pulled her sleeve over her hand and rubbed the dirty grime off the glass. She could see out now and looked down then out across the lake, there seemed no one about. The sun was on its way down and it would be night again soon. She banged on the window and shouted out. Then she tried to open it but the wooden frame would not budge, the reason being, which she could not see, was the six large screws that had been used to secure it shut from the outside. Cursing she stomped on the floor and shouted at the top of her voice as she marched over to the door again fuming with anger.

"Rose, let me out of this fucking room" banging hard and kicking the wooden door.

She felt weak still but the adrenalin rush was keeping her going, the fear was empowering her and she was scared, more than ever and the worry began to show in her voice.

Rose was sat in her chair and smiled when she heard Diana shouting from upstairs. She looked over at Travis who was sat like a little school boy on the couch sniggering like a ten year old, he rocked and held his hand to his mouth when Diana screamed out again to be let out of the room.

"She sounds real mad doesn't she?" he said to Rose smiling and laughing once.

"Yes she does, but we will calm her down, it won't take long, it never does, they come out all tough and determined but eventually they break and just collapse under the pressure"

"You know best, just let me know what you want me to do, when you want me to do it" he smiled and looked at her with his odd eyes and she smiled back at him, but it was a false smile. There was no warmth or feeling behind it whatsoever.

Diana got a sore throat and felt weak after shouting and banging on the door for about twenty minutes; eventually she just collapsed on the floor and cried out loud. She was confused and didn't understand what was happening. Taking deep breaths she just let her tears fall and it became uncontrollable. She cried out loud and shook her head from side to side in anger and fear all at the same time.

Gemma was frantic and she had worked herself up into a state looking for something that was not there, she had torn the place apart and found nothing. The police had never been back in touch or sent anyone round. She sat and didn't know what to do? She looked at her phone again then had an idea.

She searched for Diana's mother's number and was glad she had kept it all these years. She found it and rang it, putting the phone to her ear she waited but there was no answer. Not even an answering machine. She cursed and sighed out, she tried the number again, letting it ring and ring. Eventually it was answered an irritated voice said,

"Yes, who is it?"

"Hi it's Gemma, Diana's friend I was just hoping you could help me..."

"If she can't ring for help herself then no I can't help you" she said sharply.

"No, please listen, something is wrong I need your help" Gemma said quickly before she was hung up on, which was the feeling she got straight away.

"What do you mean something's wrong?" her voice was calmer but still sharp.

"She went to visit her Aunt Rose and now I can't get in touch with her, do you know where she lives now, has she been in touch with you, I am worried, I spoke to Diana and she sounded off, not herself, I just know something is wrong" the phone went silent and Gemma just heard breathing on the other end until she finally answered.

"Is this some kind of sick joke?" she said with a hint of disgust in her voice.

"No, please what is wrong I am very worried, she has not answered me back and I can't get in touch, her phone seems to be turned off"

"Listen Gemma, call the police and do it now, tell them the address, do it now" her voice was suddenly full of concern and panic.

"I don't have the address this is why I am ringing I can't find it, I just have some grabbled directions, what the hell is wrong?" Gemma insisted.

"Listen to me, ring the police tell them, we are coming over" the phone went dead and Gemma was shaking. The fear in her heart gripped her and would not let go, her stomach felt empty and she started breathing heavily. She rang the police again and waited for an answer, it seemed to take forever and she cursed with impatience.

"Yes hello I rang this morning about my friend you said you were going to send someone over, but no one has come, I feel something is very wrong and I am concerned about my friend" Gemma told the uninterested female voice on the other side of the phone.

"Who did you speak to and what is your case number please?"

"What? I don't know, I spoke to someone who said it is a missing person's case and you can't do anything for 24 hours, but listen this is serious I need to speak to someone, can you send someone round straight away please?"

"What is your name and address Miss?" the voice said still in the same monosyllabic tone.

"Gemma Sutcliff, 24 Spinnaker Road" she heard some keys being pressed.

"I see there is a ticket out already for you to receive a visit"

"When, can they come now?" Gemma was becoming annoyed at the lack of interest.

"I can't give you a time I am afraid, but they will come to you when they can, they will have a list you see and will visit when they get to you, could be today or maybe tomorrow"

"What? Fuck me" Gemma hung up the phone and threw it down on the bed in disgust.

It was less than twenty minutes before she heard a rapid knock on the outside door. Looking out of the window she saw it was Diana's parents. The knock came again and she ran down to open the door. Both Diana's parents were there looking confused but very worried also.

"Have you rang the police, did you tell them" Diana's mother said as she walked in followed by her husband who closed the door behind them, he was a tall and sincere looking man.

"Yes I have but they are not bloody interested, treating it has missing person's case until more comes to light, I might get a visit today or tomorrow"

"You should have said you think you have shot a intruder, they would have come straight around then" Diana's Dad said.

"Fuck" is all Francis said as she sat down biting her thumb nail and shaking.

"What the hell is going on, what is wrong, tell me" Gemma said sitting across from her.

"I will go put the kettle on" Conrad said going into the kitchen.

"Deinstitutionalisation they called it" She just shook her head.

Conrad came back in and sat with his wife, he put his arm around her and comforted her, he looked at Gemma and smiled then he took a breath.

"Ok Gemma listen to me very carefully, what has happened and who was in touch with Diana?" his voice was serious and his face matched it perfectly.

"She has been getting these texts from her Aunt Rose and was very excited to hear from her after all this time and even told her about things in the past that Diana loved. Anyways she asked her to go up and visit her, which she did, but the last time I talked to her she said something is not right, she was very tired and out of it, and now I can't get in touch with her. The phone is dead, I can't find the address and I asked her for it but she said it was gone off her phone, I just have a few clues, she handed him the note pad she wrote on. He looked at it and she watched him read it and noticed Francis crying to herself.

"Ok, what I am about to tell you we have pieced together over the years, he said putting the notepad down, Francis stood up and went to make the tea. We never told Diana but Rose was committed, she had a nervous breakdown and was put away in a mental hospital, it was not a nice thing to do but she had mental issues all her life. Like I said we never told Diana because she was so close to her, anyways in the nineties they closed these places and they put the patients in community care.

"Oh my God," Gemma said putting her hand over her mouth.

"It was felt drugs could take over from what the asylums and hospitals were doing, Deinstitutionalisation they called it. Well it didn't work I can tell you. Anyways it was in one of these places Rose was befriended by this other inmate, or whatever they say, patient, a woman. She seemed to be helpful to Rose and became her friend. But what she was really doing was manipulating and bullying her, she knew everything about her, asked her about her past, where she grew up, her likes and dislikes, got to know everything there was about her.

Then she started to dress like Rose and act like her, concerns were put forward but no one listened. We blame ourselves as we stopped visiting so much, Rose became distant and was given more drugs and just was not the same woman. They send these poor souls out into the world with mental health issues, and then expect them to act if they don't have anything wrong with them and just get on with life. Out in a world that doesn't want them and they find it increasingly hard to adapt to.

"That is terrible, what happened to her, is she mentally ill?" Gemma asked.

Francis walked in with the tea on a try with milk and sugar and put it on the small wooden table in front of them.

"She is dead" she simply said taking a cup, and taking a sip tears in her eyes.

"Dead, but she has been texting Diana?" Gemma was confused.

"This woman got to know everything there was about Rose, and then she became Rose acting like her, talking like her, and even told everyone that Rose was an imposter" Conrad said taking his tea, putting some milk in it and taking a drink, then he put a bit more milk in and stirred it with the small spoon that was on the tray.

"Yes, Rose was found dead, strangled but no one was to blame they said, bloody pathetic, that is what it is, pathetic, they could not prove a thing" Francis said with tremendous anger and hate in her voice that it made her shake.

"It wasn't handled properly and to be honest no one cared, but they could not pinpoint or prove who had done it, although it was obvious who had done it. This woman was dressing like Rose, did her hair the same and talked like her. The law in this country seems to protect the guilty and fails the innocent and the victims, so we did our own investigation. It seems this woman was obsessed with Rose for some reason, so whatever Rose knew she knew, all the experiences she had she knew about, she got to know her entire life, and poor Rose never suspected anything just thought she had found a friend at last"

"That is bloody ridiculous, no that just can't be, why was this not investigated, when did all this happen, who was this bloody woman?" Gemma said just as angry as Francis.

"It was several years ago that she died, but this woman was transferred there from a clinic. She had been in a few community care places apparently, she was involved in some sort of fire where her child died, it sent her over the edge, believe me we have tried and tried to get justice but no one wants to know, no one is interested, no matter who we tried to pay off. The place is closed now, they say because of cut backs, but it is because of neglect and they don't want their mess going public so just hope it will go away, no records, nothing we can find"

"I am so sorry" Gemma said wholeheartedly.

"Well you can see why we never told Diana, but now you say Rose is texting her and has invited her away somewhere?" Conrad said.

"Yes, she knew about Diana, she said she was Rose and wanted to see her?" Gemma said biting her bottom lip and putting two and two together.

"Oh my God," Francis said shaking her head and holding her hands together to try and stop them from shaking.

"Ok, so this place Deighley, where is it how far?" Conrad asked Gemma while he put his hand on his wife's shoulder to reassure and calm her.

"I tried to Google it and find it but it doesn't exist, I have no idea, Diana said she took the sign for this place, and saw a large tree with a large cemetery and a windmill, you read what I wrote that is just what she said"

"Ok, when did she leave, what time of the day can you remember?" Conrad asked her.

"Oh it was early before eight"

"Can you tell me when she got there, did she ring or text you?"

"I got a missed call from her, hold on, she took her phone and checked the time of the call, yes it was just over two hours later" Gemma said looking up at him.

"Well let's assume she arrived then, and gave you a call, I take it that was the plan to let you know when she arrived?"

"Yes that is right" Gemma nodded and breathed in and exhaled out again.

"Ok so we shall say an average speed of what fifty miles an hour, for two hours that is a one hundred mile radius, it says on your pad head north"

"Bloody hell yes" Gemma said discouraged, at the thought of it and glanced at Francis who seemed to be just listening at this point.

"Right so for a one hundred mile radius north, we have to find a very large cemetery, a windmill and, he picked up the note pad and read it again, a large tree across the road and a lake, right we have something to go on here"

"Oh my God how can this be happening to my little girl" Francis said putting her face into her hands and started to cry.

Conrad held her and comforted her, Gemma felt helpless but was determined to get something done about all this. She felt partly responsible for letting her best friend drive up there alone in the first place.

"Don't worry we will find her" she said to Francis as she composed herself somewhat again.

"Yes we will, right the police won't help until it's too late so we have to go and find her ourselves. Let's get searching for these land marks and see if we can find any or all within this radius. Have you a computer or laptop Gemma?" Conrad asked and Gemma jumped up and came out of the bedroom with a laptop in her hands, then things got moving and they started, they knew the day was ending and tomorrow could be too late.

# CHAPTER FOUR

Tucker was laid on his bed, he had been crying and the tears were still wet on his cheeks. He often had to endure the memories, there was no escaping from the all consuming power they had over him. It was a nightmare he would have for life. He wished he had the courage to stop it, to go and make it right in some way but he knew he never would have and what's more, she knew he never would have. That is why she was laughing at him from the window today. He rolled over and moaned out in agonising, psychological pain and guilt. Sobbing again he curled up on the bed and hated himself for being such a coward.

Diana was still banging on the door but she was tired and weak from all the excursion and lack of food, her stomach felt empty and was growling at her. Hearing someone coming up the stairs, she put her ear to the door and listened, it was quiet but she was sure someone was there behind the door she could just sense it.

"Rose is that you? Listen, open the door Rose, it is alright just let me out, I am not mad or going to hurt you, please just let's talk, ok" she said and listened hopefully. The lock then clicked and the door handle began to move, standing back for a moment Diana got ready to dash out and down the stairs. The door slowly opened and she then grabbed the handle pulling it open quickly, ran out and collided with Travis. He giggled and grabbed her around the waist, lifting her up off the floor. The surprise shocked Diana for a moment but then she started to struggle, he tightened his grip and then suddenly he put her down and a crashing back hand hit her across the face. She was stunned and the pain shot through her head like she had been hit with a baseball bat knocking her to the floor. Travis dragged her by her arm and she started to struggle again and shout at him. He giggled and hit her again across the jaw, this sent her head back and she suddenly felt sick and nauseated. He stood there smiling at her and she looked at his face and drooling mouth as he stared at her.

Pulling her down the stairs she was roughly pushed to the floor at the bottom, she looked up at him and saw he was giggling a silly, malevolent giggle at her. Looking around she saw Rose stood looking at her and a wooden chair in the middle of the room.

"No, no way no" she complained but her defiance was met with another blow across the head which dazed her and she could not focus. Lifting her up with an effortless exertion Travis roughly threw her into the chair. Before she could resist there were plastic bag ties around her wrists pulled tight and she was tied fast into the chair. She could taste her own blood on her lips and started to pull and panic.

"Just stop resisting and he won't hit you again" Rose said condescendingly.

"Rose, please stop what are you doing, tell him to stop" Diana pleaded but it all fell on deaf ears. Travis tied her feet to the legs of the wooded chair and she was helpless and could not move. She was scared and felt vulnerable and helpless. Travis then stood back to admire his handy work. He checked all the ties and made sure she was secure and unable to get free. The plastic was digging into her wrist a little tight and she had to stop moving her hands otherwise it dug in and was painful. He then backed off looking at Rose, she gestured him to go. He looked at Diana, grinned then went to the sideboard and took something from the drawer. He then left through the door and she heard another door open and close, further back into the house somewhere.

"Now you stop struggling, there's a good little girl" Rose said sitting down in her chair, inhaling and letting her breath back out slowly.

"Please tell me what is going on Rose, why are you doing this, you must let me go" Diana said her head still ringing from the blows she had received from Travis.

"All will drop into place soon, you will see and would have helped me, your poor Aunt Rose" she said with a smile.

"Rose untie me, let me go I do not like this, please let me go" she tried to struggle but the plastic ties dug in when she did.

"You should be thankful, the last time I was strapped up and secured to a bed I got raped and the time before I got electrodes placed on my temples and a tremendous voltage put through my head, they outlawed it many years ago but the bastards still had the equipment"

"What are you talking about?" Diana said confused and getting stressed at being tied up and unable to move, the panic was rising in her whole body.

"It is about time you know what happened to poor Rose I suppose? Well your mother had me committed to a mental institution, a hospital for the mentally insane, an asylum"

"There are no such things anymore Rose, what is this" Diana said.

"Do not call me a liar" Rose yelled, stood up and came across to her fast and easily punched her hard in the face. Her eyes were wide and she was breathing heavy and snarling. She then calmed down and went and sat back down, being all calm and relaxed again. Diane was in shock, she didn't believe what had just happened, her confusion didn't outweigh her fear and she started to shake and breathe erratically.

"Please, please" was all Diana managed to say her voice faltering as she was also doing.

"Like I was saying dear, you Mum had me committed, I was just having a breakdown but she had me put away, obviously didn't tell you. Anyways the vile things that happen to you when you are in there you would not believe it's enough to drive you mad!" she said smiling at her.

"Let me help Rose, please untie me" Diana pleaded, she looked at Rose who was staring straight at her but seemed not to see anything. Her head was slightly tilted to one side and she had a small smile on her face but her eyes were blank and had no life or warmth in them.

"They pump you full of drugs to keep you quiet, but some of the inmates pry on the other inmates, the weak and vulnerable ones, and if they are drugged up they can't really do anything about it, so they are abused, not only by the inmates but by the staff too. I learned about the drugs, I stole lots from the asylum they called the community care clinic. I was not supposed to have them but I am very persuasive and always get what I want you see. The drug that has been knocking you out is especially good, gives you headaches though if you use it too much and too often. The other things I mixed with it I have no idea what it is but the tablets looked pretty" She then stared at Rose and it made her feel uneasy. Her eyes were void of emotion and just blank looking at her, nothing behind them, nothing warm or welcoming.

"Rose, I can help you, get you help please we can work this out just untie me please"

"Do you remember when you were a young girl, you always wanted me to tell you about when I was young and what we did, do you                                remember                                that?"

"Yes, I remember" Diana thought it best to humour her and try and get her to understand and maybe loosen the ties at least.

"Well when I was young we had this cat and my little brother and two of his friends tied a make shift parachute to it, we went upstairs and threw it out of the window to see it open up and the cat glide down to the ground. But it didn't and the cat just fell out of the window onto the ground. But the funny thing was when it ran away the parachute opened and it could not go too fast because the parachute was pulling it back. Everyone laughed but I did not find it funny. I thought it was very selfish of that cat not to open the parachute when it was suppose to and let us see what we wanted" she stopped and looked like she was in deep thought, Diana shifted in the chair and felt uncomfortable and could not move out of the position she was in. She held her panic down but was struggling to control it more and more, swallowing she didn't know what to say looking at Rose motionless in her chair.

"Rose these are very uncomfortable and tight, please let me go" Diana said softly and tried to sound friendly, meaning no harm or threat.

"I hated that cat after that, it was selfish and not friendly, I had to do something about it, I hate things being unfriendly to me, so do you know what I did, I got some petrol and when the cat was asleep I poured the petrol over the damn thing..."

"Rose please let me go, why are you doing this to me, you are being unfriendly to me right now, come on now please just let me go" Diana pleaded. She was not as strong as she thought she was and was shaking, beginning to lose control, feeling trapped and claustrophobic with not being able to move. Breathing heavy she could feel the tears dwell up in her eyes, looking at Rose just sat there uninterested.

"The lighter was my fathers, he had an old fashioned bin lighter, you had to fill it with lighter fuel and it had a flint in it, and the top flipped up when you pressed it with your thumb and it turned a little wheel on the flint and it ignited the wick, don't thing they sell them these days"

Pulling at her ties Diana was starting to panic, seeing Rose talking but not directing it at her she was just sat looking down and seemed to be talking to herself and not listening to Diana at all. Eventually she looked up at Diana and smiled; she watched her pulling and struggling but said nothing and just let her panic and upset herself in the chair.

"Let me go" she screamed at her crying and sobbing as she lost control and could not stop struggling or crying.

"No need for all this, you silly girl, you are a nice girl and will make a nice baby for me so stop all this nonsense, would you like some hot chocolate and a sandwich?"

"What the fuck are you talking about?" Diana screamed shaking her head and not listening to what she was being told, she just wanted to be free of these ties.

Rose shook her head and smiled a little smile at her then stood up, she walked out of the room and left her there tied to the chair.

"Rose, Rose, get back here, you can't leave me here, Rose" Diana screamed but she knew it was useless. She had no idea what was going on but she knew she had to get out of this place as soon as she could. She pulled at her ties but it was no good she had no leverage and they were too tight, it hurt her when she struggled with them, especially the ones around her wrists.

The whole house dropped silent and she could hear nothing, not a sound. She sniffled and shook her head, her hunger made itself felt and she felt weak. Relaxing for a moment she took some deep breaths and tried to calm herself. She looked around the room to see if there was anything that could help her escape. The place was old and bare. She tried to move with the chair but it was useless and futile she could not do it. She was stuck, trapped and there was nothing she could do about it at this time. But she made herself a promise she would put up a better fight when they did finally let her out of the chair. Travis, the man with the odd eyes would not be hitting her again she thought to herself.

Dropping her head down she closed her eyes, she was feeling tired again but wanted to stay awake. Confusion was racing through her mind and fighting with the fear she had already in there, one was battling with the other and fear was winning.

Travis was out the back and had walked to the edge of the lake, he was looking at the phone of Diana's he kept flipping through the photos.

He knew he was told not to turn it on but he wanted to see, he kept looking over his shoulder to make sure no one was watching him, especially from the house. He started to grin when he saw the photos of Diana's and then some of her and Gemma together. He was making silly little noises to himself as he flipped through them. Eventually he sighed and took a deep breath. Looking out at the lake he brought his arm back and threw the phone as hard and as far as he could into the lake. It splashed once and then was gone. He stood there looking and then waved at it as if he was saying goodbye to someone. Turning back he went towards the house again. Walking past the main room window, he stopped and peered in. He could just see Diana through the crack in the curtains, her head was hung down and she looked like she was asleep, but he noticed her shoulders rising and falling as she sobbed. He smiled then giggled and carried on around the side of the house and along to the edge. He went down the small four-stone steps situated there and through a small, painted wooden door that lead into the old cellar of the house. He turned on a light switch and a single bulb dimly illuminated the small damp room. He closed the door behind him and went over the stone floor which had large pieces of cardboard boxing laid flat in it. There was a small single bunk bed and an old dirty mattress on it in the corner. Next to this was an old wooden chair he was using as a side table. Rolled up at the bottom of the bed was a thick blanket and small pillow. The walls were brick and it was cold and damp. The ceiling had drips of water and condensation on it that fell every now and then onto the cardboard below laid flat on the stone floor. When the house was in its full glory years before, this was the coal cellar and was much bigger but now it was his makeshift room and home. He sat on the bed, rocked and started to hum to himself. Thinking about the photos he had just seen he started to smile and the more he thought of Diana he giggled and then started to laugh uncontrollably. Rocking his head back as he did, he was getting excited and started to clap his hands in excitement, only stopping himself and putting his hand over his mouth but still laughing through his fingers.

Tucker was asleep, he was restless and moving his head side to said, saying "No" over and over, the nightmare was making him sweat in his sleep. He was running, running like he did that night, looking for her, he had to find her, calling her name.

"Tammy, Tammy" he shouted out running fast, he was younger and had no stick, no limp, he looked fit and active. He was searching the trees. Desperate and distressed he went on his way, the sun had almost gone completely down and it was getting dark. But he was not bothered; he had to find his little girl, his daughter. Coming down by the side of the lake he stopped and looked out across its calm water, it was alive and vibrant with life. The ducks and waders had settled down for the night, the breeze rippled the water and it was serene and picturesque, the healthy live expanse of water it used to be.

"Tammy, Tammy" he shouted, fear and worry in his voice. He searched frantically around and then saw the house, the big house and the size it used to be. A grand structure of red brick, large and full of life and character, well looked after and kept in good repair. The tall chimney stack had a slight cloud of smoke rising from it being drifted away by the evening breeze, he cursed out loud and dashed for the place. Running fast he gathered speed across the cut lawn and down the gravelled path. He slammed into the front oak door to stop himself. He pounded on the wood and screamed to be let in.

Using his fist he hit the door relentlessly, a small outside lamp came on and he noticed movement of the downstairs curtain. Then the light was turned out again, this made him angrier and even more determined, he kicked the door and pounded on it until his hand hurt and stung, shouting at the top of his voice as he did. Eventually the light came back on and he heard a noise behind the door. A clicking of locks being unbolted, the door opened a little way. He pushed and tried to ram into it but the strong chain attacked on the inside stopped him. He shouted and started to ram his body weight against the door.

He had to stop when the barrel of a double barrel shot gun came through the gap and was pointed at him, he backed off and ducked as the gun was fired and both barrels were shot. He rolled away, quickly got up and went to the side of the door with his back to the wall.

"What have you done with her, where is my Tammy?" he shouted out frantically. The door was slammed shut and he heard the bolts being put back in place. He ran to the rear of the house and tried one of the back doors, this was also locked. He moved around carefully past the windows and went to the weakest door in the house. This was the kitchen door and had a glass pane; he then used his elbow and broke the glass with two sharp hits. He reached inside and was able to undo the lock which had the large key still in it. He opened the door and dashed inside. It was lit up well from the two lights in the ceiling but he had to stop and freeze in his tracks as he saw the shot gun pointing straight at him.

"Where is she, where is my Daughter you sick bitch?" He screamed at this woman holding the gun at him, her head tilted to one side and a blank unfeeling look on her face.

"Get out of my house, or I will kill you" she said steadily.

"Well that is what you are going to have to do, my daughter is here somewhere and I am not leaving without her" he stared at her then the gun in turn. He was breathing heavily, scared and nervous but for now he was holding his space.

"She left, she is not here, she is gone" The woman said smiling at him then she squeezed the trigger letting off one barrel. Tucker dove out of the way but some of the buckshot caught him in the shoulder. He rolled about in pain but was still able to grab a kitchen chair and throw it at her. She swung the gun around and the chair hit her square on in the face. It was a good shot and a lucky shot, but one he welcomed with a grunt and he stood up seeing her drop the gun, it went off and fired the other barrel's shell as the shot embedded in the wall.

He went forward and hit her hard in the face knocking her back onto the floor, charging past her he looked around the house and started to search for his daughter.

"Tammy, are you here? Tammy its Dad" he shouted and spun around only to get a fist in the face and this woman going wild at him, scratching, kicking and screaming like a mad woman. She pushed him back and he fell trying to defend against the frenzy attack. Scrambling to his feet he suddenly felt the agonising pain in his groin as she kicked him hard between the legs. She stood back and watched him roll about on the floor in pain, tears in his eyes and a nauseating sick feeling engulfing him. Hacking a laugh, she breathed heavily and pointed at him laughing and spiting at him like a demented demon, her eyes were red and her teeth grinding as she snarled at him. He welcomed the breather and used it to his advantage, spinning on the floor he kicked at her ankles and swept the feet from under her. He used all his strength and fought through the pain he was in. He managed to jump onto her and pin her to the ground holding her hands down and using his weight to keep her there, she was fighting to get free and spitting in his face as he pushed down with all his might holding her wrists and forcing her to stay on the floor where she was. She was kicking her legs out and trying to squirm away. He was struggling to hold her so he took his right hand off her wrist and hit her hard across the face with his fist. Her head was violently snapped to the side but it didn't stop her, she still screamed and fought him, he hit her again and again and this time she looked dazed and her eyes looked glazed over. Her struggling had stopped and she was semi conscious. He took large breaths and rolled off her, holding his groin he managed to get some feeling back and the pain to ease. He struggled to get up and was unsteady on his feet, not thinking to tie her up he staggered out of the kitchen area. Smelling a horrid smell he went into the room and looked around. It was a large, well furnished place with a small fire burning in the fire hearth. He looked around, went out to the backroom, opened the door and the smell almost knocked him out, he had to put his hand to his mouth to stop him from gagging.

Never smelling anything like it before he backed out but then stopped, he saw the baby cot in the middle of the room so he took his handkerchief from his pocket and used it as a mask. He walked over to the cot and looked in, he was instantly sick and had to back off and spew over the floor, he breathed in but the rancid smell made him sick again. The sights of the rotting baby's corpse made him sick and almost pass out. The poor infant was dead and decomposing in the cot, a horrid smell and stench came from it and had filled the room sticking to the furniture and walls. He shook his head in disbelief and rushed out of the room, he turned and was

92

attacked once again by this woman and she tried to kick him again but he was too quick and managed to get back out of her way. She screamed at him and cursed a bombardment of obscenities at him as she came forward lashing out and kicking at him. Dodging and trying to get his breath back, Tucker backed up and then without warning just dashed forward barging her out of the way. Falling back she reached out to grab his leg as he ran past, he was by the stairs and without thinking dashed up them in a blind panic. She stood up and gently looked in the room where the dead baby was and she gently closed the door as you would after you had just put a child to sleep for the night and didn't want to wake them again. She disappeared into the kitchen for a moment and came back with something in her hand. Looking up the stairs she wiped the blood off her face that had come from her burst nose where Tucker had punched her. She slowly started to hum to herself and climbed the stairs one at a time looking up in front of her as she did. Her eyes were narrowing and she had a look of pure evil and hate on her face. She could hear the painful cry and uncontrollable sobbing from the far back room, she knew where he was. A smile came across her demented face and she slowly walked across the upstairs landing. The door was wide open and she could see Tucker on his knees crying into his hands, a small boy with odd eyes was sat curled up in the corner chewing on his sleeve of the small red shirt he was wearing. She took no notice of him and just stood there looking at all the blood on the floor and this broken man grieving and shaking unable to control himself.

On the bed was a young girl, her legs open, her eyes the same, a look of pain and anguish on her frozen face. The blood had been soaked up on the sheets of the bed and they were saturated deep red. It was a hideous sight and one Tucker would take to the grave. He was shaking, inconsolable and could not take the sight of his daughter dead on this bed in front of him, all the blood and the remains of an umbilical cord coming from her. The eyes still open and the mouth dropped open too, it was a heartbreaking sight to behold, by the side of her head was a small bundle wrapped in a pillowcase, this too was red blood stained from the newborn. Moaning out the pain he was feeling he sat and rolled over on the floor then the realisation and the anger took over and he spun his head around to this woman stood at the door looking at him smiling a vicious smile.

"What have you done, you sick bitch" he shouted getting to his feet.

"She was unable to deliver, the next one will be better I am sure" she said and with that she brought the lighter fuel bottle up and pressed it hard as the petrol inside hit Tucker in the eyes and temporarily blinded him. As he backed off and staggered about, she carried on squirting him with the highly flammable liquid, stepping aside and pushed him back out of the room. She then took the bin lighter she had in her other hand and flipped the top to ignite the wick and threw the burning lighter at him. It instantly engulfed him as the lighter fluid caught and burned rapidly. He screamed and held his hands to his face blindly staggering about, bumping into things and the flames catching his clothes afire as he did. The woman slowly picked up the fallen lighter and went back into the room and closed the door. The flames started to ignite the floor where a lot of the fluid had spilled out. He knocked a picture off the wall and tripped up, rolled and hit his head at the top of the stairs dazing him. The flames caught the small cloth hanging off the small table at the top of the stairs and soon the fire was taking hold. The heat and pain in his face was becoming unbearable and Tucker tried to stand. He was still blinded as he stumbled and fell down the stairs rolling down painfully and out of control. He landed awkwardly and snapped his leg with a sickening cracking noise. The bone had broken and it was sticking out of the left shin as blood began flowing out quickly.

Screaming out in pain, he patted his face to dampen the flames and he pulled himself across the floor as the fire was catching hold of the old dry wooden interior quickly. He pulled himself along and bit his tongue with the agony and hurt. He didn't know how he did it but he got to the backdoor and managed to roll outside. He screamed out and grabbed his leg. His eyes were watering and he was partially blind but he got out and pulled himself clear. He could see the house was catching on fire more and flames were coming out of the upstairs window as black smoke rose into the sky. His heart pumped hard and the fear was like a pincer grip on his entire body. Looking back and seeing the figure of this woman at the doorway looking at him, she suddenly screamed an insane scream and came dashing and running straight at him with evil and madness in her eyes and face.

He awoke screaming, crying and rolling over in his bed, it was his nightmare for life and it never got any better or any easier. He would have to relive it and do so until he took it to his grave. He sobbed and rolled over, his hands covering his face, he knew what she was and now he was too much of a coward to do anything about it. The whole situation was made worse that she got away with it, the fire destroyed all the evidence, the body was never found, he knew what she had done with it but even though they sent divers down to the lake the body was never found. She was committed, the young boy disappeared and Tucker had to try and rebuild his life. But the sight of his daughter would haunt him and it was something he never got over. His life was empty and he was a broken, sad man who just went down to the lake all the time. He knew that is where his daughter was even though they never found her body he knew, and would always know. Even though no one else believed him and everyone had forgotten now, he knew and would never forget. He would sit at the lakeside most mornings talking to her, asking her for forgiveness. He was putting himself through the pain and anguish of it all, over and over. Causing him to drop into depression and hate himself. People got to know him as being the weird, old man with the stick. Some who knew what had happened left the area. Most people did over time as the place started to die. Forgotten and neglected it fell off the map, what was once a great little beauty spot was now a dead place no one wanted to see or visit. He had to suffer alone and the woman, the cause of all his pain and self destruction was laughing at him from inside that house. The same house where it all happened and the same house where his life had ended. Not caring about himself or looking after himself he was ill and he didn't care, he could feel the darkness creeping around his body. Eating him away physical and mentally but he just didn't care. In fact he would welcome it, just a pathetic mess, a complete failure and coward. He judged himself harshly but this was the only way he knew how to judge himself. He rolled out of bed and went to the bathroom, then into the kitchen he put the kettle on to make himself a drink. Everything he did was slow and his face had a constant sadness about it. He just stood motionless waiting for the water to boil in his kettle. This was how his whole life was now played out, he was just waiting to die and would welcome the day it came.

# CHAPTER FIVE

Gemma was comparing what she had found on her phone to what Conrad had found on the laptop, they came next to each other and analysed their findings.

"Ok I googled windmills and lakes, and have a possibility" Gemma said.

"Yes I have one too, I googled lakes and cemeteries and found a large cemetery but no mention of any lake? There is a windmill close by also, let me see yours and I'll compare it to where mine is. There doesn't seem to be a place call Deighley, either Diana said it wrong or maybe you misheard her, but we can't use it"

They looked on the laptop and on Gemma's phone, they wrote the two possibilities down on the notepad with the original directions Gemma got off Diana. Francis was sat still looking worried but let them both do what they were doing.

"It looks like these two places are not that far apart, this must be it, she must be in this area. We can go to both places and see what we can find" Conrad said throwing his pen down onto the table and holding the notepad in his hand.

"Let's get going" Gemma said standing up and heading for the bedroom to get changed.

"Hold on, it is dark and we need to be able to see where we are going. It is alright going to the place now but it will be late at night, we can't see anything. We are looking for landmarks, a large tree, a windmill, it will be better in daylight. Let's get some rest since we're exhausted and we can set off first thing in the morning" Conrad suggested.

"No, I am going now, I will book into a place around this area and set off first light, minutes wasted here could be a matter of life and death up there" Gemma firmly said and went into the bedroom to get changed.

"She is right, we have no idea what is going on or how much time Diana has? We have got to get up there" Francis said. They all agreed and the decision was made.

Diana was still and had calmed down but was very uncomfortable in the chair. Rose had not made an appearance since but she had heard someone in the house moving about. It was dark and the only light she had was the low wattage bulb hanging down from the dirty ceiling. The fear rose as the door opened and stood there was Travis, his odd eyes looking at her. He was not saying anything and he just looked back and up the stairs then came into the room, closing the door behind him.

"Go away, what do you want, go away" Diana shouted at him. He put his hands up and gestured her to be quiet, he put his finger to his lips and asked her to be quiet.

"There is no need to be frightened from me" he said sitting in the chair Rose had sat in.

"Who are you, let me go out of this chair, please I promise not to tell anyone" Diana pleaded with him and tried to work out the best way to handle this chance she might have.

"You know there is a large tree over yonder, big oak, its branches come right over the road it used to be used to hang witches? Did you know that witches used to be here in the old days and they used that tree to hang them? That is fact and on some nights they say you can hear then gagging to death" he told her this information as if it was the most important thing to say to anyone.

"Why are you doing this, please just let me go ok" she asked him as nice as she could fake.

"I live here and I have been working on this place ever since I was a little boy. I rebuilt most of it, got things from here and there you know, and when she came out, she got it really done up good, plumbing and electricity. It is a lovely house isn't it? Big and grand, it used to be much bigger and they don't make them like this anymore"

He looked around the room and nodded his head admiring the place, and then he looked at Diana again and smiled at her. She could smell his disgusting body odour, it was like foul onions and it was making her feel sick.

"Will you please let me go, or loosen these, they are very painful look at my wrists" she said nodding to the deep red marks going around them from the tight plastic ties.

"Sorry but I can't do such a thing, not yet but I will, I can promise you that. Did you know there are secret rooms and a secret cellar? Well there used to be, its all caved in now after the fire, but we could hide things there and no one would ever find them" he giggled and put his knuckles in his mouth from his right hand for a few moments then took them out.

"Can you tell me why you are doing this, please just tell me" she said losing her cool but trying to control herself as much as she could.

"I remember when the fire started, I was told to take someone down there, she had not been well and I had to stay there with her and her little pillowcase, not sure what was in the pillowcase but I stayed there for a long time. She never moved or said anything, neither of them did, but I did as I was told and stayed there until it was safe to come out, I always do as I am told you see" he smiled and looked proud of himself.

"Well if that is the case then I am telling you to let me go since you always do as you are told, you just said so! You're not a liar are you?"

"But you are not her, she always tell me, I have to do what she says, I have to" he looked nervous all of a sudden and started to fidget.

"Listen I won't tell her, it can be our secret ok, just come and undo these horrid painful ties for me, you can do it, it's easy for a good man like you" she said hopefully.

"You and me are going to be friends, she said so, we are going to be very good friends" he smiled at her then started to giggle. He started to look at her body up and down, he started to get a lustful look and his mouth started to dribble from the corner. His eyes got bigger and he licked his lips and took a nervous breath.

"No, no that is not right or true, no you can't touch me, not at all no" Diana insisted and started to struggle at her ties again. The pin in her wrists was getting worse and worse but she didn't care, she had to get free. He stood up and started to gesture with both hands for her to stop and calm down. He looked at the door and started to become nervous.

"Shhhh, please be quiet" he said.

"No, get away, leave me alone, no" she screamed out loud and started to try and move the chair as she did. He came over and put his hand across her mouth but she shook her head free and screamed out again. Becoming angry, he backed off and headed for the door but froze as it opened. Stood there was Rose, she was glaring at him. He buckled under the pressure instantly and dropped to his knees, looking up at her with his hands together as if he was praying. She stared him down for a few moments and then nudged past him into the room.

"Go make Diana some hot chocolate Travis, do it now and make it strong" he immediately got to his feet and ran into the kitchen. Rose came in and sat in her chair. There was no pain in her actions, no sign of old age and she sat down easily.

"You can't do this Rose, you have to let me go" Diana said and found it weird that she was actually glad to see her at that moment in time.

"Don't be silly dear" Rose said and seemed to change back into this old frail woman again who sat in the chair looking at Diana, she had a little smile on her face again.

"Who the hell are you?" Diana asked sternly.

"Your Aunt Rose dear, don't you remember?"

"Aunt Rose would have never done anything like this to me; she was kind and a good woman"

"Yes I am kind and a good woman"

"Tying me up and like this, keeping me prisoner is not being kind and a good person"

Her face changed and she glared at Diana for a moment and then she seemed to settle again and not rise to what she said. She moved and acted like a pain had shot through her body.

"Arthritis is very painful Diana dear" she said her eyes saddened and painful.

"Being strapped in a chair to tightly is, as well" Diana said looking for signs and triggers. She was trying to understand and maybe work on Rose in some way to her advantage.

"Do you remember when you were young...?"

"No I don't I don't remember at all" Diana snapped trying her luck.

"You always used to like me to play that tune on the spoons do you remember, I told you my dad taught me to play them, you loved that didn't you?"

"No, that was my mum, when you were both girls she liked you to do that not me?" Diana said and suddenly everything started to hit her at once, the realisation of it all. She took a large intake of breath and sighed out nervously. Rose stood up and came over to her slapping her hard across the face over and over, without saying a word. It stung and she screamed out in pain as her face went red and struggled in the chair. Rose then stopped and went to sit back down; she looked at Diana and smiled again. Rose sat there looking at her and it made Diana nervous. Saying nothing she just stared at her and the blackness of her eyes and the coldness of her heart could now be seen by Diana more than ever.

Shortly after, Travis came in the room with a mug of hot chocolate. Diana at first refused to drink it but they both forced it down her. They held her mouth open and poured it down. Rose punched her in the stomach as she tried to struggle, it winded her and she swallowed a lot of chocolate. Eventually they made her drink most of it and Rose sat back down. She told Travis to leave and he did so. Diana was panting and her top and front was covered with hot chocolate, it had burnt her skin on her neck where it had been spilt. She knew she had swallowed a lot and knew she would be out cold soon. There was just nothing she could do about it now.

"Do you know that society doesn't care about people, did you know that? If you can't contribute and give them what they want then you are expendable. They don't want to know about you. They call it progress or cost saving but really it is just getting rid of what they see as a liability and something that is costing them money" Rose said looking down at her hands in her lap.

"Why are you doing this to me, I have done nothing wrong?" Diana said her tears coming and her fear rising inside her.

"No, you probably haven't or you think you haven't, you are a nice girl and will make a good vessel for my child. Plant a seed in the garden and the seed will grow, I can't have children you see" she said looking up at her slowly.

"Child, Vessel? No Rose no, please, no" Diana was barely holding her panic and hysteria back. She could feel it bubbling just under the surface ready to burst out at any moment.

"I remember when they took everything I had, they took away everything, no one helped me, no one wanted to help me, I was totally alone. Put away behind locked doors, beaten, raped and abused for a long time. But then I fought back. Society had turned its back on me"

So I turned my back on society, they had no idea how to run these facilities so I used that to my advantage. I used their ignorance and overconfidence against them you see. Let them think they have you where they want you but in fact it's the other way around" she breathed in and let the breath back out slowly.

"We can sort this out Rose, please let us just try, please I have done you no harm" Diana felt her courage drain away and the worry and dread take its place. She was stuck and she knew it, and had no idea what to do to get out of this situation.

"I got very good at it, letting them think they had me where they wanted me, it was a case of putting them into a false sense of security. You would be surprised what I got away with in the end, just a matter of knowing who you can use and who you had to humour and let them think they were in charge" she smiled and then looked at Diana. She just looked at her for a few moments and then her face seemed to change from normal to twisted as she was looking at her. The eyes widened and the glare she was now giving her increased and the lips even turned up slightly. Her whole expression changed and it was frightening to watch. Diana didn't like it and she started to shake and become very nervous. It was like a completely different woman had just changed in front of her eyes. The transformation was not a good one, Rose stood up and came over to Diana and stood in front of her, without warning she punched her in the stomach and it made Diana lose her breath and winded her instantly. She could not breathe and tried to double over as much as she could in the chair. Rose grabbed her hair in a twisted fist and continued to slap her face hard back and forth first with her back hand then the palm of the same hand over and over. Diana screamed out and lost control, the fear and pain destroyed her nerves and she just had to take what this woman gave, she had no choice. It was numbing her face and she felt swelling already, she was crying and had never felt such pain or fear in her life and just wished it would stop.

Suddenly Rose stopped, she let go of Diana's hair and her head flopped down, blood dripping from her cut lips and busted nose.

108

Wiping the blood off her hand onto Diana's top she then sat back down in the chair. She seated herself and got comfortable.

"Yes like I was saying, you are the garden for the seed then I will have my baby back. It will be nice and friendly and not cry all the time, be a good baby. My last baby was not a good baby as it made noise all the time and would not stop crying. But one night I stopped it from crying" she stopped talking and seemed lost in thought for moment. Ignoring the painful moaning from the battered Diana she just started to hum to herself and rock back and forth in the chair. Diana could not move, her head was pounding and she felt dazed and numbed. Blood was dripping from her mouth and nose and she could see it but could not move. She just watched it stain her top and jeans as it dripped and soaked into the fabric. Her ears were ringing and she felt so sickly. The throbbing in her face and head was getting worse and she could feel the bulging of her lip as her eye seemed to be closing. Eventually the hot chocolate started to take effect and the pain and numbness started to wear off as she was being consumed by the drugs in the hot chocolate, soon she was out cold and slumped in the chair.

"Travis" Rose shouted and the door instantly opened where he had been sat outside.

"Yes I am here" he said eager to please.

"Untie her, take her up to the room then tie her back up so she can't move or escape. Keep her clean as well, wash her, I am sure you will like that, get her out of them clothes and use some she brought in her bag to dress her. I do not want to see all that blood and mess all over the place. Do it now Travis!" she ordered. Without any hesitation, he came forward with a small knife and cut the plastic ties around her feet and wrists. He then threw the lifeless body over his shoulder and hurried upstairs. He was going to enjoy this very much.

# CHAPTER SIX

Gemma had indeed found a Bed and Breakfast and they all had booked in and were in their rooms. Their plan was to start first light and go and check on what they had found out, hoping their research would come up with something. Francis was quiet, she was just holding together, Conrad was being strong for them both but he too was struggling somewhat. He was scared and worried about Diana, he knew what sort of woman she was with and he knew anything was not beyond her. They settled in and went to bed as it was already late. As he held his wife, Conrad remembered the conversation he had with one of the orderlies he paid off at the Community Care Centre. He had spoke to him alone and not told Francis the whole story, he felt she had been through enough with losing her sister.

The off duty orderly and Conrad were in a pub they had arranged to meet in. They both sat in a corner with a pint of beer each which Conrad had bought. The place was quiet and it was how they liked it. Out where no one knew them, somewhere safe and away from nosey people with big ears and bigger mouths. He was an older man about sixty and wanted his working life to end; he was worn out and had enough, he was not bothered anymore. The whole system had failed him and over the years it had gotten worse. He was very experienced and very knowledgeable but it didn't seem to account for anything. He was constantly struggling and battling with red tape bureaucrats and he could see what was wrong but he never seemed to get anywhere when he brought the problems to light. He was sick of his job and sick of the system that employed him, a system that wanted him deaf, dumb and blind.

"Well I managed to get a look at the file" he said slowly and in a low voice.

"Well you know whatever you tell me is strictly between us, you know that, I will never involve you in anything, you have my word" Conrad reassured him.

"It better be, I am putting my whole fucking life on the line here, the fact is they should not be letting these people out into society. Not only can society not cope with them, but they most definitely can't cope with society. These drugs they are giving them are just flat liners; they just hold the line down a bit that is all. Stop the medication and what do you have. A fucking lunatic that is what, I have seen it, I know what they are capable of"

"It must be a hard and stressful job" Conrad said sipping his beer.

"You have no fucking idea, none, no one will, while it is all covered up like it is"

"Covered up?" Conrad asked confused.

"Yes they shut the asylums then the mental hospitals and the institutions; we have community care now, fucking legalised drug houses. The medication helps a lot don't get me wrong but you know we are not dealing with normal human beings here" he took a large drink of his beer. Conrad could see he was a burnt out man and someone who wanted out of the system he had been a prisoner too for so long.

"So they just keep them drugged and hope for the best?"

"These people are not as stupid as they look; I have seen mental patients at genius level, calculated and methodical in what they do. Dangerous, very dangerous, they know the system and play it. These young, wet behind the fucking ears psychotherapists these days have no chance, they just eat them alive. They come with a bit of paper saying they are smart and can do the job but they have no idea, in fact a lot of them should be on the other side of this fence"

"What do you mean? I don't understand, they are there to help surely?"

"Help, ha don't make me fucking laugh, I have been in this job all my life, over forty years and I have seen it all, psychopaths, sociopaths, murderers, hopeless insane maniacs. All the bloody lot, you name it and nowadays they have these know fuck all, straight out of university lot. Do everything by the book and make the biggest mistakes we have to sort out, or they are just left and society has to pay. Like some poor fucker who comes on the wrong end of one they have let out saying he or she is fine, cured" he shook his head and took another large mouthful of his beer.

"That is insane" Conrad agreed taking a drink of his own beer.

"Good choice of words, well I am just bitter and sick of the system and society that just wants to throw them all on the scrapheap and save money. Because that is what it is all about bloody money, not caring for people, no let's see how we can save money? So many slip through the net and are out there now, just waiting like a bloody time bomb ready to explode, but it is not just the ones we knew about, they're all over the bloody place, society is full of them. Do you know where the biggest places you will find psychopaths? I will tell you and that is politics and banking, and that is a fact. You have to understand what a psychopath is, they are born that way, a sociopath is different, circumstances can cause them to do what they do, abuse as a child or constant bombardment of a bad situation, they can be driven over the edge, but Psychopaths are born, it is imbedded already in their brain" he stopped himself and looked around the pub, he didn't want anyone hearing him.

"I am sorry, that is bloody unbelievable" was all Conrad could think to say at that moment.

114

"Don't be, it will only get worse and the cover ups, the lies and the white wash will all get bigger. Anyways, the reason you are here. I saw her file; yes she has been in care since she was arrested for killing her own child. There was a fire and a local man accused her of kidnapping his pregnant daughter but no body was ever found and she was not convicted of it. The house was destroyed by fire and was put under state ownership until she came out, or was fit to be put back into society as they put it. Helen, that is her name, was moved around a lot, everywhere she was sent, things happened but she was always too clever to have the blame put on her. If you ask me she manipulates others to do her own dirty work, Helen loads the bullets but someone else fires the gun if you know what I mean. Anyways she did befriend Rose; she did obviously have an obsession with her for some reason. Rose was due to be released, she was getting out but this bitch managed to stop it, she was giving Rose some drugs to keep her under control, how the hell she got the drugs I don't know, your guess is as good as mine. Anyways from what I can see, and think what happened was she started to spread rumours about Rose, bullying other inmates to accuse Rose of things she was not doing. The poor woman had no idea, she should have been walking free but it got pulled and poor Rose was in no fit state to fight it in any way. Her psychotherapist was fucking useless and knew nothing, like I said one of these university types with no experience of the real world, spent all their life in a fucking classroom and thinks the world is the same way"

"The fucking bitch" Conrad shook his head and was annoyed and ashamed at the same time. They both took a drink of their beer and Conrad sighed out shaking his head.

"Sorry for the bad news but you did want to know, and as for Rose it was sure as hell this bitch that killed her, we all knew but again the investigation didn't want to know"

"No please carry on, anything you can tell me" Conrad insisted.

"Yeah it would be bad publicity especially now they were methodically closing all the places down saying they were not needed. We can just release these people onto the streets and into a world they have no idea how to survive. Just give them drugs and say nothing"

"Do you know what happened to her, where she is, this Helen?" Conrad asked.

"Nope, sorry, I did not get access to that part of her file, no one will, they protect them like fuck, you will be very and I mean very lucky to find that out, in fact I bet her file will go missing, it happens all the time"

"What do you mean, how so?"

"The dangerous ones are not always where they say they are, not to panic people they give them false identities"

"No, that's rubbish that can't be, surely not" Conrad said shaking his head unbelievingly.

"I am telling you, files go missing all the time, the whole fucking system is corrupt, you have no idea what goes on, no one does, that's all I can tell you I am afraid"

Conrad never saw him again, he never told Francis the whole truth about Rose should have been getting out, and he looked down at his wife asleep on his chest and smiled at her. He just wanted all this to be over and have no more drama and bad luck for his family. He hoped to God they would find Diana and that she and Francis would make a conscious effort to make up and get on better now. He wanted to go to sleep on a positive and hoped he could actually get some sleep. He suddenly felt very tired and closed his eyes.

Gemma was unable to sleep. She was busy still trying to locate these clues she had from Diana. She found pretty much what she already had and just seem to be going in circles, there seemed no more. Putting her phone on charge she finally laid back on the bed. It was a quiet, little pub and although it was lovely looking it was all lost on her at the moment she was oblivious to her surroundings. When they had booked in, she asked the owner about these landmarks but they seemed not to know of any of them, which was very disheartening to say the least. She had already taken a shower and was laid on the bed; she was going over the last night she had spent with Diana and the next morning before she left.

Going over it all just in case she had missed or forgot about something, trying to remember their phone calls and what was exactly said. It was making her anxious and worried thinking about it, and thinking what will happen if they just can't find these places. What if they are in the wrong part of the country? What if Diana never rings or texts again? She had to shake the thoughts from her head and stay positive, she just wanted the phone to ring now and Diana to say everything is alright she is coming home. She picked up her phone and made sure the ringer and notification sounds were up to maximum then closed her eyes and tried to rest but knew she would not be able to. Her thoughts drifted off to better times when she and Diana were together. The holidays they had been on, the times they had shared and everything they had been through. Not sure if it was making her feel better or worse she laid there and continued to hope and remember for the rest of the night.

Diana was waking up and was feeling sick, her face ached and was throbbing; she had a swollen closed eye and a nasty cut lip. She coughed and tried to swallow, she felt weak and her head was thumping from the inside out. Tied at the wrists and ankles, she was on the bed on her back, the sun was just coming up and the

118

light was coming through the windows. The curtains were still on the floor; she closed her eye and opened it again. Waking up the best she could, she looked down and noticed she was dressed in a light summer one piece dress she had brought with her. Moving a little she realised she had no underwear on and the only thing she was wearing was the light dress. Shaking her head she started to cry. The thoughts running through her mind about what could have been done to her while she was out cold, she probably would never know, would she ever want to know? Her hands were tied together in front of her with the plastic bag ties again, her ankles too but she could lift her knees up and work her legs up and down against each other. This gave her a little hope, she might have a chance. She kept trying to pull her feet free one at a time, up and down against each other, working the tie free she hoped.

Rose, or rather Helen was dying her hair, it was no longer the grey she had pulled and tied back, it was dark brown and cut shorter. She looked a different woman, still thin and gaunt but she would soon put her weight back on. Starving herself had made her look older and weaker than she actually was. Helen was still agile and much fitter then she made out, not as old or as weak, she was good at fooling people into thinking what she wanted them to think. Looking like, what she actually was, an older version of the woman who had set Tucker on fire all those years ago. She was washed and dressed in more modern and suitable clothes for her age, a light blouse and jumper with a pair of trousers, and a small pair of black boots. She walked strong and steady and went out of the door. Walking around the house she went to where Travis had hid the car and using Diana's keys she got in and drove away. She smiled to herself and was happy thinking things have worked out good for her and soon she would have what she wanted, her own baby, one that would be nice and not cry and make a lot of noise. It made her insane mind happy to think about it and she had no second thoughts whatsoever of the pain or torment she would cause to get what she wanted. Driving steady she headed for the nearest village and wanted to finally get herself some proper food and other supplies. She settled into driving this car and liked it; it had been a while since she had actually driven but soon got used to it again. Although it was very early morning the sun was coming up fast and the day was breaking out and blooming once again.

Gemma was up, packed and ready, they had decided to have a quick early breakfast and head out. The breakfast was eaten quickly, they settled the bill and then Gemma pulled up on her phone where they were.

"Ok, so we are here and the windmill, is about five miles or so down this road, shall we start from there?" she said sitting in the front seat looking at Conrad who was driving.

"Sounds good, let's go, give me directions" he said as they drove away.

"That landlord was very unhelpful, did you notice?" Francis said from the backseat.

"Yes, he was, didn't want us there, probably don't like strangers around these parts" Conrad said pulling the car out of the car park and heading off where Gemma pointed.

"No bloody way to run a business, I am sure he knew where we wanted to be, but just would not tell us, why would people be like that?" Francis said sighing out and shaking her head.

"We will find her don't worry, we will be close, we have to be, all the landmarks are around here, so it's just a matter of placing them right and we will find where she is" Conrad said trying to comfort his wife, who he could see was worried and anxious.

"Turn your next left" Gemma told him looking at the map on her phone to see where they were going and heading hopefully to Diana she prayed. Looking around the quiet countryside she thought it would be a nice place in different circumstances, but never now, because of why they are here, the pain and upset will always be associated with this place from now on.

"These bloody roads are narrow" Conrad complained as he drove along the small road and could not see around the next bend in front of him, hoping no car would be coming the other way.

"Let's hope this is the same windmill Diana talked about" Gemma said biting her bottom lip in thought and worry in case they were in the wrong place.

"I am sure it is, we will find her" Conrad said in a strong positive voice which somehow made the two women feel better. It was what they wanted and needed to hear. He drove around the bend and was pleased the road looked clear ahead of him. Gemma kept an eye on where they were and directed Conrad accordingly. Francis was holding it together in the back and was glad they had come along this early like Gemma had insisted yesterday. She said a silent prayer for her Daughter and one for the both of them, making the decision never to fall out or argue with her little girl again after all this was over.

Diana's ankles were sore, she had made them bleed, the plastic ties were digging in but suddenly it snapped and her legs were free. She uncontrollably laughed out as she did it, so happy she started to cry. She stood up and looked around the room. Feeling a bit unsteady she shook her head and carefully went to the door. She slowly tried the handle but it was locked. Taking deep breaths she was finally able to see straight and not feel so tired but her head still pounded on her shoulders, she fought through this and went to the window. Peering out she could see the place looked deserted. She tried the window again with her tied hands but it was useless and it would not budge. Going to the bed she lifted the mattress and was pleased her thoughts were correct. It was an old bed so still had the old fashioned bed springs where the mattress sat. She put her hands on either side of one and pulled the plastic bag tie which was around her wrists over and started to try and work it loose. Pulling and pushing to and fro, she worked the plastic on the metal spring. She kept looking at the door as she worked. Pulling it and stretching it, her wrists were burning and bleeding but she would not stop as pure fear and adrenaline kept her going. She was pulling hard and suddenly it snapped, her hands were free, standing she rubbed her sore wrists and stretched up and out. She was so pleased to be free and now all she had to do was get out of this house. The window was a no go she thought could not risk smashing the glass they would hear her. Settling for a fight when they came in, she looked for some sort of weapon she could use. The wardrobe, she walked over and opened the one door on it and saw what she wanted. The clothes pole across the inside was of the old fashioned type so it was a strong round metal bar. This would be her weapon of choice and she set about taking it out. It was not too difficult and she soon had it in her hand. Her weapon was ready to smash anyone who came through that door. She stopped and thought for a moment would she be able to hit Rose, but she decided she could just push past her if need be, the person she would be hitting would be odd eyed Travis. She stood behind the door and waited, taking the time to breathe and fight her hunger and thirst.

"Where is it, it should be here?" Gemma said disheartened they had stopped and were looking out across the landscape but couldn't see any windmill.

"Does it say it is here?" Francis asked from the back.

"Let's just drive a ways down it might just be off bearing sometimes. Satellite, bloody things, used to use maps in my day" Conrad half joked but he was worried just like the others.

They all breathed out in excitement when he rounded the next bend; there in front of them was a wooden windmill. They all laughed and looked at each other.

"Yes, good old satellite navigation system" Gemma said smiling at Conrad.

"Ok let's say she drove past here, to the right is a large Cemetery?" He said and Gemma instantly started to look on her phone map. They carried on and unbeknownst to them, went straight past the small road that would have taken them straight to Diana. The road that had the fake sign of Deighley on it when she passed but Travis had taken away now. The mood was lifted in the car and they had hope once again. Gemma could not see the cemetery and was trying to get her bearings right. By the time she did the satellite took her a completely different way, they headed for the cemetery but from the opposite direction and it would take longer to get here.

"I do not understand why we can't find Deighley, I am sure that is what she said" Gemma told Conrad as he drove along to her directions.

"I don't know, let's not worry about that now I can feel we are close, I just can feel it" his optimism kept the mood in the car alive and on a hopeful high. It was what they all needed, each having their own thoughts and fears but all pulling together to try and find Diana. They all wanted the same and they all would do anything to see her safe again, the positive attitude of Conrad kept that alive for them and they appreciated it very much.

# CHAPTER SEVEN

Diana was still stood by the door, getting agitated and started shaking again. She wanted out and was sick of waiting. She tried the door handle once again but it was not going to budge. Looking over to the window, she walked to it and had a serious inspection. She thought maybe she could get down if she did smash it and got out? The answer to her dismay was no, it was just too high up. Cursing she hit the frame with her hand, there was no other way out of the room, she was stuck. But at least she now was free of her ties and she had a weapon. Walking back to the door she put her ear to it and listened, she still could not hear a thing. She looked to see if her metal pole in her hand could force the door open but it was useless. She had no choice but to stay here and just do a surprise attack on whoever entered the room then make a run for it. The headache in her skull was getting worse, she was hungry and very thirsty, feeling dehydrated she went and sat down on the bed, the strength was draining out of her and she started to feel the fatigue set in. Putting the pole down for a moment she rubbed her wrists and then her ankles which were very sore. Moving her feet around to get her circulation back she did the same with her wrists and hands, although it was painful to move them because of the sores. It was just good to have the freedom of movement again. Shaking her head she knew she must stay awake and alert, this was going to be her only chance and she had to take it. She went to the door again and got ready. Her face was throbbing and she could feel the tightness of where it was swollen. Her eye was closed but she could almost see out of it now, the other eye was fine and at least that was something to be grateful about. She stood ready and just thought about how she had got herself into this mess. The next time she would listen to her friend and let her come with her, she would never be this trusting again, no matter who it was. Taking a deep breath she held her weapon hard and tight in her hand, she was ready and was going to give it her best shot, whenever that shot came.

Tucker was up out of bed and made his breakfast. He was looking ill and feeling the same. He was walking slowly and relying on his stick heavily, more so than normal. Heading out the front door, he walked slowly down the road. It was quiet and still, unnaturally so. He remembered when the birds sang around here, when it was a fabulous and beautiful place to live. The more people left and the more new people came, things got forgotten and when the place died it was never the same again. Walking down the road he was alone with his thoughts but also alone in his life. He could not help remembering when he used to bring his daughter down this road. She would hold his hand and skip along, always happy and always smiling. He tortured himself everyday thinking about her, he could never get it out of his mind. The good times they had always made him feel good for only a moment because then he remembered how she ended up. Then the pain stabbed his very heart and soul and the self pity and self destruction always followed. He struggled down the road lost with his thoughts and his tormented memories. Turning off he walked down the once lovely green pathway, flush with greenery and flowers. He could never explain why everything died, he never really understood. He just knew it did, the lake had his daughter and it was weeping for her and everything else followed is how he explained it to himself. He had died that day and so did everything else when an angel and perfect person is brutally taken the way she was taken. When his wife died, Tammy was all he had and all he lived for. She was going to get the best of everything and anything she wanted. He closed his eyes when he thought about that night she was attacked near the house on her way home. They never caught the attacker but she was violated and became pregnant. He pleaded with her to get rid of the child but she would not and could not. He stood by her and would have looked after the child with her. All he wanted was her to be happy and have the life he never had. Coming to the old log, he sat down by the Lake. He looked back towards the house and sadness filled his already drooping eyes. He looked out across the lake and was silent and motionless, just looking, just watching.

Helen was in a nearby village, it was one that kept itself to itself and she welcomed that. She went into a local store and started to get what she wanted. The car was parked outside and she was the first one in the store that had just opened its doors. Ignoring the woman who opened the door for her she went straight in and began to search for what she wanted.

Unbeknownst to her passing along the same road but not noticing Diana's car parked up was Conrad driving and listening to Gemma who was looking at her phone working out directions. Francis was in the back her eyes down and her hands in her lap, she was having memories of all the times her and Diana had argued in the past. The regret of it was overwhelming and she was holding back her tears as she thought of the wasted months and years they had when they were not talking or had fallen out about something. Although it seemed significant at the time just seemed trivial now and unimportant. She remembered her as a child and how lovely and happy she was. Conrad was the proudest father alive when she was born; he spoiled her and gave her everything. It must have been hard for him to see them both argue, she now thought about it. He was always caught in the middle and always tried to see both sides. But that is an impossible position to be in sometimes and he always handled it as well as he could. Remembering all the times he had asked her to go and make up, to ring Diana, and all the times she had been too stubborn to do it. Wishing she had done now she held back her tears and hurt. The regret she had and the pain she was now feeling accompanied with the rising fear in her stomach in case they could not find her. But she had to stay positive, Conrad had told her all along that was the best way. She was trying to take his advice today but she was finding it difficult. The natural pessimism she always had was beating her down and she was afraid it was starting to win the battle. Breathing in deeply she tried to keep calm and looked up and out of the window seeing what she could, trying to help the others to find what they were looking for, a large tree across the road or a cemetery, or the Lake.

"Ok if I am reading this right, there should be a cemetery here, just anytime here now" Gemma said looking out for it and checking on her phone.

"There we go, yes, yes, yes" Conrad said with an excitement and exhilaration in his voice. He pointed ahead and they all laughed out with just as much enthusiasm. There was the cemetery; it was coming up on their right. Conrad slowed and pulled up to a stop. They all looked at the huge size of the place spread out in front of them.

"There it is the bloody cemetery, well done Gemma" Francis said not able to hold back her excitement and relief at seeing the place, knowing they were a bit closer to her daughter.

"Thank you, we are making good progress. This must be the place, it must be" Gemma said with excitement looking around out of the windows.

"Why are there no people about, nothing the place looks dead" Conrad pointed out.

"Well it's still early, we can ask someone when we see them where the lake might be" Gemma said looking down at her phone.

"Ok we have two choices, he said looking ahead at the road, we can go straight, or make this turn here to the right?"

"Well I would say if we go straight we will end up where we have come from, so it's got to be that way, according to my phone map anyway. If we take the straight road it doubles back and we end up where we have been so let's try that way down there" she pointed to the right turning road. Conrad followed her lead and headed off down the road, it was narrow and he didn't like these conditions. He drove steady and Gemma kept looking at her phone.

"There is no bloody lake though, what the hell" she said looking up and out of the window, but she didn't want to get disheartened because it was going well.

Diana froze for a second she heard a noise, she put her ear to the door and listened. Yes there it was again, someone was moving about in the house she was sure of it. She took a deep breath, this could be it, trying to swallow and then held her pole up in her hand gripping it tight. The ready position was there and her heart was pumping fast. Hoping she would be able to do it she started to shake. She had never hit anyone before let alone having to attack them, but then again she had never been in this position before, fighting for her life like this. Taking another deep breath, she blew it out again quickly making her cheeks puff out. Her hand was sweating and she was feeling the nervous empty feeling in her stomach. But still focused she listened and stood poised and ready. Looking around the room and back to the door, she heard another noise and it made her jump. Her nerves were giving her a fight and she was struggling to keep them under control but she knew she had to. One shot is all she was going to get and she had to make it a good one. The pole was held high and she was as ready as she was ever going to be. Listening as hard as she could, the silence was almost buzzing in her ears. Trying to pinpoint and work out what the noise was she was hearing exactly. Where it was coming from and who it might be. She was breathing heavy and could hear her own heart pumping away in her chest. Stood she wanted the door to open, almost trying to will it to open; come on she was ready and waiting. The noise then was louder, she held her breath as she heard someone coming up the stairs, was this it, was this her chance, she held the pole ready. The footsteps went over the wooden floorboards and towards her door. Gasping as they did she could feel herself shaking uncontrollably then the footsteps went past her door and she heard another door opening down the way. She was breathing erratically and shaking, not knowing what to do she just stood there and waited, it was almost the time for her to act, to do what she had to do. Sweat was dripping off her and she felt a sickness coming into her stomach. The fear gripped her and the adrenaline speeded her heart up, her nerves were only just holding together, she was ready and waiting.

"Oh my God, look" Gemma said pointing ahead.

"The bloody oak tree, it's massive" Conrad said.

"Oh my God" Francis screamed out holding her hands to her mouth she started to sob shaking as she laughed nervously.

"We are close, very bloody close, come on get going" Gemma said with her excitement showing too, she had to let out a nervous laugh.

Conrad sped up and headed past the tree, under its large branch hanging over the road, he went up the steep hill in front of him and then they all gasped and cheered in the car as they saw the water ahead, the lake.

"That is not on the map, how bloody strange is that?" Gemma said shaking her head. Slowing down Conrad stopped at the junction. They now had three choices left, right or straight ahead. He turned his head to look at Gemma who was looking at her phone. She looked up and pointed ahead.

"Are you sure?" Conrad said going ahead after checking both ways.

"No, but let's head for the water, she is near the lake, we just head for that, come on we must be here, this must be it" she eagerly looked around swivelling in her seat to look out of every window and searching for a house of some sorts. They drove past the cluster of trees and the open wooden bar gate not realising. They were lifted, their spirits were high and they could feel they were in the right place. Somewhere near was Diana and what they had to do now was find her. Going slower Conrad could see the road headed off out the other side. He slowed down more and stopped. Looking back he shook his head saying.

"I think we have missed something, somewhere"

Diana was sweating, shaking and gearing herself up to the most important decision in her life. The footsteps came back, they were outside the door. The lock was undone and the handle turned. This was it, she stepped back and was ready to hit down with her weapon. The door opened and in marched Travis with a cup in his

134

hand. He saw the bed empty and his mouth dropped open. Diana brought the pole down as hard as she could across his head; it bent with the force of it. She hit him again this time across the shoulder. But to her horror he didn't go down, he just took them and looked at her. Diana couldn't believe it, this was not how it was suppose to go, he was suppose to drop down. She tried to hit him again but he caught it in mid air and yanked it out of her hand. She screamed and ran out of the room in blind panic. He raced after her and they fought on the landing. He was bleeding from his head and grunting at her while they fought. Diana did everything she could, scratched and punched and kicked like a wild cat. Screaming she wiggled out of his grip and dashed for the stairs but he was quicker than she anticipated and he kicked out at her ankle and she lost her balance. She stumbled and to her shock, rolled head first down the stairs. Hitting them hard as she did, shocks of pain bolted through her body as she hit different parts of her body on the wooden steps as she rolled down. When she hit the bottom with a hard and painful thud she was temporary dazed. She noticed him stomping down the stairs after her and she tried to get away but the pain in her body had other ideas. She could not but tried to stand, her leg was weak and her ankle sprained. She screamed out and fell back down in a heap. Travis with an inflamed look of anger on his face grabbed her by the hair and started to pull her back up the stairs. She grabbed his hands, kicked out and tried to stop him but he was too strong for her and started to climb back up dragging her with him. Screaming out in defiance she turned and punched him between his legs twice in succession catching him hard in the testicles, he cried out and let go of her to clasp his groin in pain. She rolled back down the stairs and hit the bottom again. Crying she tried again tried to get to her feet, she managed to limp and struggle to the front door. She reached up and just did not have the strength to reach the top bolts of the door. Sobbing she collapsed back down in pain and agony that was ripping through her entire beaten and battered body.

Travis was rolling about on the stairs and then looked over at her with a vicious hate in his eyes and a snarling face as he stood back up.

Just then Diana heard and felt a loud knock on the door. They both froze for a split second, not sure they had actually heard it. Then it came again, two loud knocks and a voice she knew, her jaw dropped and her heart raced up like it was going to burst.

"Hello anyone home?" Conrad said stood outside the door.

"Dad, dad, quickly please" she screamed and tried again to stand to open the door but Travis was there pulling her back towards the kitchen. She screamed at the top of her voice and struggled all she could.

Conrad heard her, so did Gemma and Francis. They all pounded on the door but it was solid and not going to budge. They shouted out her name and became desperate, Gemma going to the windows but couldn't see inside. Francis just stood there shouting Diana's name, she was becoming hysterical and couldn't help herself.

"The back, I'm heading to the back" Conrad shouted and raced off around the side of the house. Gemma gave Francis the phone and told her to call the police. She then went and ran after Conrad. Francis started to look and struggle to see the numbers, and then she noticed there was no signal. She cried out and still kept trying.

Conrad was kicking the back door in when Gemma got there she could see the anger and power in the man and was impressed, he seemed meek and quiet but when needed he knew what to do and would do it without hesitation. He kicked and put all his weight behind it eventually the door gave and the glass pane shattered as he fell through with the momentum of it, he looked up and froze. Gemma dashed in after him and screamed holding her hands to her mouth. They saw Travis, his arm around Diana in front of him and a large kitchen knife in his hand which he had dangerously at her throat. Diana was beaten and dazed, she was almost unconscious.

"Stop, you just wait there, I do not know who you are but just stop, calm down" Conrad told him in a commanding but non threatening way. Gemma started to slowly edge to the side of him, she was horrified to see her best friend is such a beaten state.

"Travis moved the knife and threatened to push it into Diana's throat" grunting out as he did.

"Stop, no" Conrad said freezing and Gemma stood still too.

Travis was looking at them both in turn and moving Diana about as he did, he was still in pain from his groin and his head was still bleeding over his face. He started to blink as the blood hit his eyelids.

"Just take it easy, just let her go and we will leave" Gemma told him her hands up in a non threatening manner. Travis turned to her and spat out at her, growling and shaking he was beginning to panic and didn't know what to do. Conrad was looking at the knife; it was just too close to Diana's throat for him to make a dash in at this moment.

"Yes, just calm down, we will not do you any harm, just let us take her to the hospital, ok just put the knife down, please" Conrad said edging a little closer.

"We mean you no harm, just let her go and you can be on your way" Gemma said to him taking his attention away from Conrad, who she could see was just waiting for a chance.

Shaking his head Travis grunted and was confused, he didn't know what to do.

They both looked at him; he was perplexed and didn't know who these people were, they were edging slowly closer to him. Diana was scared and dare not move she could feel the knife's blade on her throat. Travis pulled her closer, the smell from him was nauseating and she had to cough as the stench from him got into her mouth and nostrils. He backed up to the small cooker and banged into it as he did. Gemma was coming around the table from the left and Conrad was edging to the opposite side, he was concentrating on the knife and waiting on his chance. Travis shouted out some inaudible word at them in anger and held the knife out towards Conrad, he looked over at Gemma and at that precise moment Diana plucked up enough courage and strength to hit his arm and stomp on his toe. He yelled out and Conrad was there and was quick. He grabbed the wrist of Travis controlling the knife hand and with the other he hit him hard on the jaw, then they started to struggle and fight. Diana screamed out but Gemma ran forward and pulled her away. The girls backed up and watched as Conrad struggled and fought with Travis, they knocked over the small stove and the gas pipe was pulled from its holdings, gas was now leaking into the kitchen. Travis was strong and was not easy to control. Gemma dashed forward and kicked him hard on the leg then ducked away as he swiped out at her with his fist. Conrad head butted him and hit him again as hard as he could.

"Get out" he shouted to the girls and then he kicked at Travis as he fell to the floor. Standing up quickly, Travis backed off and still had the knife in his hand. He was now stood at the back door blocking their exit. He was snarling and snapping at them like a mad dog, the blood dripping from his face and he had madness in his eyes.

Everyone froze for a moment, and then Gemma pulled Diana out and they headed for the front door to escape that way. Conrad followed and they ran but suddenly stopped in their tracks looking in horror at the image they were confronted with at the front door.

Stood in the door way was Francis looking petrified, she had a knife to her neck and stood behind her holding her the same way Travis had held Diana was Helen. Diana shook her head and cried shaking, finding it hard to stand. Gemma kept hold of her and steadied her friend the best she could. Helen stared at them all in turn and then nodded her head once towards the front room. They could smell the gas coming from the kitchen but it didn't seem to faze Helen at all. They all slowly edged into the main room and Helen walked in using Francis as cover and the knife so close to her throat that it was drawing blood. Francis was scared beyond her comprehension and it was the most frightening time of her life.

"Calm down, just be careful" Conrad said to her holding his hands up to her.

140

"Shut the fuck up and get over there" Helen snapped at them, they all backed into the room.

"Just take it easy" Conrad told her trying to calm the situation.

"Sit on the floor, all of you. Sit on your hands on the fucking floor now" Helen barked at them and they all did as they were told. She then walked into the room still using Francis as her shield and weapon of power while she had the knife to her neck.

"Why are you doing this?" Gemma asked her.

"Travis, Travis, are you alright?" Helen shouted out towards the kitchen.

"Yeah, yeah I am" his voice came back. He dare not come in because he knew Helen would be mad at him so he stayed there in the kitchen even though the gas was leaking out.

"Well, watch the back door, you stupid man" Helen said sarcastically and disgusted.

"Please" whimpered Francis as she shook with fear and felt faint.

"So what do we have here, intruders into my house, broke in, caused damage, attacked my servant, disgusting wouldn't you say" Helen asked in a composed manner.

Diana looked at her and was disgusted with herself for falling for the charade, she held onto Gemma and started to get her nerve back just a little bit.

"Just let her go, we can sort this out" Conrad said from his position on the floor. Helen knew what she was doing having them all sit on their hands as it stopped them from rushing her.

"Shut up you stupid fucker, so let me guess you are little Diana's daddy and this here in my arms is mummy? Yeah must be, your sister was such a weak pathetic soul you know" she said talking into Francis's ear close and tight, while looking at Conrad and smiling.

"Stop, stop this please" Francis said in a whimper.

"Yeah Rose was an easy target, told me absolutely everything about everything, stupid old cow she was. You just dump her away and leave her to be savaged upon by people like me, how horrid you are! Now you come here and want to rescue poor little Diana, the little spoilt brat who thinks she is Miss Prim and Proper" Helen looked at Diana with disgust and hate in her eyes, then she turned her attention to Gemma. She smiled at her and looked her all over and nodded and smiled.

"Look you can let us go, there is no need for this" Conrad pleaded.

"Do you want me to slit this whore's throat, do you? Shut the fuck up" Helen snapped at him with a venomous spite, she then looked at Gemma again and smiled. "Yeah I was going to use that little whore there, but I think you will be a better garden for the seed to grow, yes you can give me my baby back I think, Travis, will like you I am sure"

"What do you want?" Gemma asked her holding onto Diana who was holding her back and feeling a bit stronger now she had her family around her.

"What do you want" Helen mocked her with a silly voice then looked at her with contempt.

"There is a gas leak back there, we need to get out of here" Conrad said but regretted it after the words had left his mouth. Helen looked at him and pushed the knife a little further into Francis's neck, the blood started to come out and Francis panicked and was shaking and whimpering. Diana shouted out and Gemma had to hold her back from dashing forward.

"One more stupid remark to insult my intelligence and she loses her jugular vein, all over the fucking carpet a red gushing fountain of life just cascading away like a fucking waterfall. I have seen it happen, it doesn't take too long. People like you make me sick living your little lives thinking you are all perfect and better than everyone else? Well sorry but no you are not. How fucking easy was it to get that stupid bitch to come here, poor old Aunt Rose texts you and you come running after twenty years, really? How fucking stupid, I only tried it in the million to one off chance and there you are running here to help little Aunt Rose"

"It is gas in here, gas" Travis shouted from the kitchen where he was stood by the back door as he had been told to do, because he always does what he is told.

Without warning Helen was about to slice Francis' throat when she heard a noise behind her, she turned and saw the stick coming down at her. Before she could stop it, it had struck her hard on the head, Tucker stood there lifting the stick again to hit her where she had fallen. Conrad dashed up and grabbed Francis pulling her out of the way.

"Get out, go away never come back" Tucker shouted at them, then he hit Helen again with his stick, she seemed unconscious on the floor. He watched as they all dashed from the house and out to the front. Standing there he was crying as all the horrid memories came back to him of the last time he was here. He looked down at Helen on the floor and saw where she had dropped the knife. Conrad told Gemma to get everyone into his car, he then came back in and saw Tucker stood looking up the stairs and the tears running down his face.

"Who are you, come on we must get out of here" Conrad shouted to him.

"You go now, I am going to end this place, it will never hurt anyone again, leave now, go" Tucker shouted at him and Conrad felt he was compelled to do as he was told, he wanted to get his

144

family safe and that was his main priority. He left and jumped into his car, looking back and seeing Diana and her mother hugging in the back. Gemma was staring at him from the front seat then shouted at him.

"Get the fuck out of here man, what are you waiting for go, go" She screamed at him and he did as he was told racing away.

Travis came dashing from the kitchen and pushed past a surprised Tucker. He went into the living room and saw Helen sprawled out of the floor, blood coming from a nasty gash on her head. He turned and ran towards Tucker, he was unsteady himself from the blows he had taken earlier but he plunged the knife in his hand deep into Tuckers belly, pushing it hard and in with all his weight and might. Tucker jabbed his walking stick hard into the face of Travis, the end of the stick hit him in the eye and he screamed and staggered back holding his face. Tucker mustered all his strength and courage, dashed forward as he barged Travis down and got past him. He stumbled into the kitchen and headed for the back door. Bleeding badly he held his wound with one hand and used his stick with the other. He had to stop by the door and take a breath and he was not sure he could go on; he was weak and losing blood. He could hear Travis screaming and bashing about blindly inside. He staggered out of the door and limped awkwardly away but fell down to his knees, the blood seeping through his fingers onto the ground in front of him. He didn't hear the other car start up around the front and race away because he had no idea that Travis, in his blind agony, feeling his way along the walls had hit a light switch. The internal spark you sometimes get with these old brass switches was enough to ignite the gas that was saturated in the air from the leaking cooker.

The explosion was tremendous, it took half of the building with it and the fire ball ignited and engulfed the rest. Travis was torn into little pieces as the explosion ripped through the building, relentlessly destroying everything in its path. Tucker was literally lifted off the ground and thrown yards away with the blast's impact and shockwave. He screamed out and landed on his side, he rolled away and moaned out his pain. Looking back he saw what was left of the house, it was burning and would not be saved this time. He smiled and was glad, finally he had done it. He strangely felt better in his last minutes of life, he dragged himself with determination he didn't know he had. Struggling across the ground and leaving a trail of blood, he painfully carried on and was not going to stop. He kept going and eventually after an agonising crawl he had reached the lake. He was on his belly and just looked out across the water. He knew his life was now over and all his pain would be gone. He was about to close his eyes when he noticed something. There in the water, a ripple and movement. He was confused and didn't know what was happening. He tried to focus and saw that the water seemed to part, something was there. He looked and his heart, that was racing and pumping so hard to keep him alive, suddenly slowed and he felt calm. He smiled and reached out. His daughter was stood there in front of him smiling at him all happy and just as she used to be, joyful, young and beautiful. His eyes filled with tears and he said sorry to her in a weak voice. She reached down and took his outstretched hand, kneeling in front of him she stroked his forehead and smiled a loving and caring smile.

"Everything is alright dad, don't worry nothing is your fault, I love you so much" she said holding his hand. She then kissed it and he felt the pain, the worry, the dread and the guilt all lift from him. He smiled and laughed out he was so happy and looked into her loving eyes then passed away. He died a happy man at last, a forgiven man and a man now at peace. No one would know what happened here at the Lake, no one would ever know, but Tucker was at peace at last and that was a wondrous thing.

# CHAPTER EIGHT

They heard the blast when they were driving away but didn't look back, Conrad driving fast and heading down the narrow road. They had made it, done it, escaped. Gemma looked back and could see both mother and daughter together, hugging and comforting each other. It was as it should be a family pulled together in crisis.

"Thank you so much Gemma, we are forever in your debt" Conrad said glancing over to her.

"Don't be silly it was a team effort, we have her safe that is the main thing, now we must get away and to the bloody police, this is going to take some explaining"

"Well let's get safe and away from this bloody place, I do not trust anyone around these parts to be honest" Conrad said slowing up as he was approaching the junction.

Just then they all jolted forward as they were rammed from the back. Screaming Diana and Francis held onto each other while Gemma was thrown forward. Conrad looked in his mirror and saw Diana's car coming up again He put his foot down and the car chase had started. Helen was in Diana's car and driving fast and close to Conrad's rear bumper. They drove fast but it was much too fast for these roads. Helen stared unnaturally and intensely at them from the car. Her head leaning forward and her hands gripped so tightly on the steering wheel that her knuckles were white. She had her foot to the floor and was hitting Conrad's car repetitively. Blood was coming down her face and it was a million miles away from the old lady that Diana had come to see a few days before. She was right up on the car and thrust herself forward every time the bumpers were close and then followed through ramming the car.

"Hold on, just hold on, put your belts on" Conrad shouted. He dropped a gear and put his foot down, racing off and gaining distance with his more powerful car. The girls all did what they were told and belted up. Looking out of the back window Diana was crying wildly.

Her mum had her head down and holding Diana's arm tightly. Gemma looked at the door's rear mirror and could see the car coming up on them fast. Conrad slowed down to take the sharp bend in front of them that was coming up fast.

"Fucking mad bitch" Gemma said to herself but said it out loud not realising.

Again they were hit in the rear, throwing them forward in the car. The front of Diana's car was crushed and damaged but it still kept coming. Conrad put his foot down and was round the bend then sped on leaving the smaller car standing; it was no match for his more powerful car. Helen kept going as she was not going to give up and she followed, staring intensely out of the windscreen at them as she drove.

"Drive dad, go, go faster" Diana screamed at her father as she saw the car still following them. Luckily there was no other traffic about on these small roads but Conrad worried about the single track road coming up soon. If he met something coming the other way there were in big trouble. He looked in his mirror and saw the car still coming. He gritted his teeth and drove on; slowing down because of the road winding around in front of him, the last thing he wanted was to get ditched. He knew where he was but still trying to figure out where to go.

Francis just closed her eyes and held onto Diana's arm. Diana hugged her mother and they stayed tight together shaking and trying to take strength from each other.

"Hold on" Conrad shouted, he could see the car coming up fast. Then it hit, a loud bang could be heard and they again jolted forward, but the impact had engaged the airbag in Diana's car. Helen was hit back in the face by the inflating bag and she lost control of the car. It weaved off the road and down into a ditch, cracking something off the front and then hot steam came from the under the bonnet. The car was wrecked but Helen was not, she kicked the side door open and rolled out. She stood up and shook herself down as she looked down the road.

"Ha, yes, fucking beautiful" Gemma screamed and they all laughed with relief in the car as they realised what had happened. Conrad slowed down to a safer speed but was still going pretty fast. Diana lifted her mother's head up and hugged her tight. Francis hugged her back and then looked her in the eyes,

"I am so sorry, please forgive me" she said crying and shaking in Diana's arms.

"I just love you mum, I am the one who is sorry for getting you all into this" Diana said wiping her face and wincing at how sore it was, in all the excitement she had forgotten.

"You are safe, that is the main thing, safe and you have Gemma to thank" Conrad said looking at her through his rear view mirror.

Diana came forward and Gemma leaned back and they hugged for a long minute.

"Thank you Gem, thank you so much" Diana said crying her eyes out.

"Anytime, just no more visiting bloody Aunts eh?" she smiled and they all laughed as a way of stress release.

Helen was walking down the road with a quick march on and she didn't seem to feel the cut on her head. She looked older than she was and knew she needed to gain some weight, get her strength back and change her appearance. She was already planning what she was going to do but first things first. She walked quickly and just kept staring ahead, she was waiting for a car to pass and when it did she would get it to stop. Whatever she wanted she would do, without any apathy or thought for others, they were not important. Only she and what she wanted was important. Nothing or no one mattered, why should they? This was about her and her happiness, no one else's. She marched on and kept going, she knew how to look after herself and had done it all her life so nothing was different today.

Conrad drove as far as he could, he thought they were far enough away now so he stopped and took his phone out of his pocket. He gave it to Gemma to ring the police and tell them to meet him at his house. He then turned around and faced Diana and Francis who were both hugging each other. Do you want to go to the hospital baby, how are you?" he said to Diana wanting to make sure she was alright.

"No, no let's go home please I am fine, no, I do not want to be alone" she said in a panic.

"She is coming home, no bloody hospitals, she is coming home" Francis insisted. Conrad smiled and reached back, he put out his hands and they all held each other's hands tight.

Gemma called the police and explained as much as she could to them like where the place was located. She told them a bit about

Helen and told them to go check the car on the side of the road and tried to describe where it was to the best of her ability. Conrad took the phone off her and said in a stern voice that he wanted to meet them at his house. He gave the address then his name and told them to hurry, he was on his way back down now and it was urgent. He pressed the button turning the phone off and put it back into his pocket.

"Is she dead, did anyone see?" Francis said as they started to drive off again.

"I fucking hope so, the mad psycho bitch" Gemma felt compelled to say.

"They will find her, either way, no one worry about that, you are all safe now"

"You should have told them where she was, so they can go and get her" Francis told him.

"They will get her one way or another; let's just get away from this bloody place and home and safe alright?" Conrad said heading out towards the main road ahead.

"She will be picked up, and I hope they never let her out again" Gemma said.

"I am so sorry, sorry to everyone" Diana said then burst into tears again, she felt bad and horrible for causing all this; Francis put her arm around her and comforted her little girl.

Gemma smiled and was so glad it was all over, she relaxed into her seat and sighed out.

"I want to really thank you Gemma! You have been great and a real friend to Diana. If there is anything I can ever help you with, never hesitate to ask" Conrad told her.

"We made a good team, you hit and move pretty good for an old man" she said smiling at him, he glanced over to her and smiled back, shaking his head.

"I take a lot of vitamins"

"Well I will have to start taking some then I think. What a fucked up situation all that was, you just don't know who or what is living out there, and who was that old man, where did he come from?" She said just remembering about Tucker.

"Yeah, I know, bloody glad he turned up whoever he was, I tried to get him to come but he said he wanted to end the place?"

"Well I hope he did, never want to see that fucking place again, a sunny beach and a lot of drinks is where we are heading in the future, no more bloody country trips, right buddy?" she said looking back at Diana who was quietly resting her head on her mother's shoulder, she just smiled at her and said nothing.

"Sounds lovely, we will be home soon and we can all start to forget this nightmare and get on with our lives" Conrad said with his optimism as usual.

"I hear that, sounds bloody lovely to me" Gemma said and was so pleased it was all over. Knowing now she had to start to rebuild her best friend, something she would do no matter how long it took, no matter what it took she would never leave her again.

It did take an hour but Helen did get a lift. Avoiding the police helicopter she saw flying overhead at one point and taking note of the sirens she heard in the distance. She still managed to look and act vulnerable and fragile on the side of the road when she heard a car. She started to walk aimlessly down the middle of the road, a little woman bleeding and not knowing where she was, fragile and in need of help, who wouldn't stop for her.

A couple on holiday picked her up, they were young and driving along when the woman told her boyfriend to stop and pick her up, he was not happy about it but did it all the same. Helen thanked them in her little, brittle old lady voice. Telling them she didn't know where she was, her car had broken down and she started to walk but just got lost. She was so tired and could they take her to the nearest village or town. They agreed and the woman sat in the back with her trying to look at her wound. As soon as they were going again, as soon as they were settled, Helen took her chance and pulled the knife out she had hidden on her person. Leaning forward and thrusting it into the driver's neck, she then turned and stabbed the woman several times in the stomach then once in the eye. She kicked the woman off her as she hysterically fell forward. The car veered off and stopped suddenly, the driver scared and confused. She leaned forward and calmly stabbed him again in the side of the throat. Screaming he panicked and fought to get out of the car managing to open the door and fall out onto the road holding his throat, the blood pumping out at an alarming rate. He rolled over making a gargling noise and then stopped moving and was dead. Unaffected Helen opened the door and got out. She walked around the car and pulled the woman out, dropping her onto the road and leaving her where she fell. Wiping some of the blood from herself, she went to the man and searched his pockets taking his wallet. She then got into the driver's seat and got herself comfortable and familiar with the vehicle. Seeing the woman's bag in the foot well she reached over and saw there was a purse and phone in there, then closing the door she slowly drove off heading down the road. The fact she had just killed two innocent people did not bother her in the slightest. She left them there dead and bleeding out, she had something she needed and wanted to do and nothing or no one would stop her. Driving faster, her face was expressionless and she reached down to put on the radio. She tuned it through a few channels to get a bit of music and a song she liked then dropped the driver's side window down and drove on, relaxed and comfortable. She hummed to the lively song that was playing on the radio and rested her arm out of the window. The breeze was warm and the sun was up high now, it looked like it was going to be a sunny day. Glancing down she noticed all the blood on her top and in the car. Shaking her head she looked annoyed at it but paid it no more attention. She was starting to feel hungry and hoped there was a suitcase with their clothes in the back so she could change into something else if not, she would have to figure something else out. Not worried about it, she carried on and took some deep breaths of air. Turning off the road about half an hour later she headed for the country track she knew would be deserted as she had been there before. Stopping the car, she looked around seeing it was a deserted place then got out of the car; going to the back she opened the boot. Luckily for her there suitcase was in there. Reaching down she opened it and looked at the clothes. The woman was bigger in size then she was and the clothes didn't really suit her stature but she did find a few things she could manage to wear. Changing there and then by the side of the car she stripped down and put the clothes on from the suitcase. Taking a dress from the suitcase she went and used it to wipe a lot of the blood up inside the car and some on the outside just so she looked a little less conspicuous. Looking at the other stuff in the back, there another holdall bag with all his clothes, some sort of mp3 player thing she didn't understand, his toiletries and also the woman's toiletries in a little bag. Taking what she wanted and needed, she emptied the holdall bag out and filled it with what she could use.

Cleaning her face with some wet wipes she found and her hands too, dressed differently and not covered in blood anymore, she got back in the car and drove away.

# CHAPTER NINE

It had been a very challenging, tough and draining five weeks. So many questions so many things that had to be explained and proven. So many nightmares to relive, feeling they were not believed and having to go over it all again and again. Their stories being questioned and crossed checked with each other's stories. Conrad got a very good layer for them and he helped and depleted a lot of the pressure they were under. The interrogations and the bombardment of questions over and over eased as the picture emerged of what happened and were proven. The evidence from the house was not a lot, the fire had destroyed the whole place and the body parts they found could not be identified as they were that badly burnt and in pieces. The old man was found stabbed by the lake, he was found out to be a local called Tucker who they were able get information about and the local police helped with that. The stories he had told them and the reports he used to file over and over about his daughter. Eventually the lake was searched again and they did in fact find the remains and bones of a teenage girl and of a new born baby. This all collaborated with Diana's story somewhat. The two innocents found stabbed on the side of the road was still an ongoing investigation, no one saw anything and no one wanted to help in the area. They were all scared and strangely tight lipped. It was a tight community and the legend, the old house and lake had run deep.

There was country wide search put out for Helen, on the news, in the papers and the internet. Conrad had been there for Francis who was now on medication for her nerves and mental state. She had refused psychological help. Gemma was helping Diana to get back to normality as best she could. Moving in with her for a while she helped her cope when she woke up screaming from a nightmare, she never left her side and always comforted her. A panic button was installed that Diana could hit and the local police would respond immediately but it didn't do much to calm her nerves. She was in constant fear of everything and refused to go outside. The doors were always locked and checked that they were, at least ten times a day. But slowly she was getting better. She stopped going to therapy and relied on Gemma to pull her through. Feeling the sessions were doing her more harm than good, she let Gemma be her therapy and it worked much better for her. The months passed and things were getting easier. Diana lost her job and had to rely on her parents to help her with things. She didn't want to move back home but knew she would have to go get a new job again soon. It was not fair asking others to help her all the time.

Knowing Helen was never caught played on her mind the most, knowing she was still out there somewhere. Being assured by the police and her psychologist that Helen would probably be out of the country or moved on to someone else did not convince her she was safe. Feeling patronised a lot of the time, she knew what she knew and knew what she saw in that house. The experience will be with her until she dies, and being told everything will be fine, was not helping the situation. Gemma didn't patronise her, she was bluntly honest and said if Helen ever comes back they would be ready for her and kill the bitch no doubt. In a macabre way this made Diana feel better than being told by a therapist all will be alright and not to worry. Being told to relive it and not let it have a hold on her, not to be a prisoner of her bad experience just annoyed her and she had to leave. She also did her bit to help her mother, who was hurting in many ways about what happened. She called her everyday and they became close again and this was the best therapy her mother could have wished for. She was constantly beating herself up over putting Rose away in the first place all those years ago, blaming herself and getting depressed about the fact.

Conrad still could not believe it all happened, how Helen could hold all that information all that time and was able to do what she did. Why was someone like her ever allowed to be set free? He had an endless stream of questions and he never got real answers. It always came up against bureaucracy and red tape over it, just like he had been told by the orderly that talked to him back in the day. He remembered him saying they cover things up, they send dangerous people out into society just to get the places closed down. Medication helps them now, not the treatment they got in the asylums, don't need the asylums, they don't need mental institutions. Conrad could see and understand what he was trying to say back then. It only takes one to slip through, to make it past them and all havoc can erupt. People's lives destroyed and no one wants to take responsibility. What would they do if they caught her, where would she go, back into a mental hospital? He constantly asked himself these questions and never could get the answers.

He was driving on his way to meet Gemma, they had decided to meet for lunch and they often did to talk about how mother and daughter were doing. They had become good friends and although Conrad had known her for a long time before, they had never really met and talked properly in all that time. It was this tragedy and horrifying thing that brought them the friendship they had now.

He pulled up and pared outside the pub they normally met up in, he locked his car and walked towards the doorway. A boy on a push bike raced across the car park and almost hit him. He was wearing baggy clothes that didn't seem to fit him properly and a baseball cap. He was keeping his head down racing the bike past him and Conrad had to jump back to avoid getting hit. The boy seemed a little unstable on the bike but he rode away off down the road. Watching him go he noticed Gemma's car pulling up, he smiled and waited for her to park up and get out. She smiled back and locked her car coming over to him. They walked into the pub together. Conrad got the drinks; they always had the same so he knew what to order. They sat in their usual place away under the window that overlooked the car park.

"You looking rather gorgeous today" Conrad said in a friendly complimentary manner.

"Oh, why thank you kind Sir, you look rather dashing yourself" she said smiling at him.

"So how are things, getting better I hope" he asked taking a sip of his beer.

"I think so, Diana has an interview tomorrow did she tell you?"

"I think she told Francis yes, I am so glad for her, and you for getting her the chance. It's where you work isn't it?"

"Yeah it is only a junior position but I am sure she will be great in it and there is room for scope, as soon as they see what she is capable of they will promote her, I am sure of it"

"Well you are a great and true friend Gemma, we all thank you so much for what you have done and continue to do"

"No worries she is my best friend, she would have done the same for me I am sure" she said smiling and taking a drink of her white wine.

"The only good thing is it has brought Francis and Diana back together, they seem stronger than ever. Francis needed it as well, she is killing herself over Rose and everything" he shook his head and sighed out.

"It is not her fault she can't blame herself surely?"

"I keep telling her this, but she is her own worst enemy, blames herself for letting it happen and she should have gone and seen her older sister Rose more. We just could not take her in at the time, and there was young Diana to think about. It was horrible decision to make but we had no idea any of this would happen, it was supposed to help her that bloody place not cause all this"

"Well I am sure she will eventually realise it Conrad, she has a good man in you and I am sure Diana will help her along too. Don't worry yourself about it, you need some support too, all you seem to do is help others and keep everyone's spirits up" she said with a concerning voice seeing a hint of sadness in her otherwise normally optimistic look.

"Yeah I am sure, she just worries if she'll ever turn up again? If Rose told her everything then she more than likely knows where we live"

"Right I see, well if I ever come across the psycho again I will rip her fucking head off"

"Wow Gemma you are violent today, but I am with you on it one hundred percent" they both took a sip of their drinks and continued chatting. The young lad on the bike had returned and was in the car park watching them; he was keeping his head down and seemed to be taking note of their cars. He then rode off again a little unsteady but good enough to get him about.

"It will never make sense to me why the hell she was ever allowed out, I mean surely they could see, she was taking over Rose, she was much younger and acting much older?" Gemma said shaking her head looking at Conrad.

"I know it doesn't make sense does it, I have talked to people who worked there and one told me they just wanted to empty the places, cut backs and just to save money, they don't care about people anymore" He took another large drink of his pint.

"But why throw her out, back to her house, they must have known, she looked very old and wasn't, is that not a warning bell?" Gemma said shaking her head.

"Well she probably changes her appearance to suit her circumstances, she was just looking old to convince Diana who she was, but she might be completely different now, like you say she is nowhere near the age she acted or looked, she is very clever"

"Well that's a blood worrying thought, I just hope the mad bitch is gone, and gone for good"

He held up his drink and they touched glasses and smiled then both took a long drink.

"Can you keep a secret" Conrad said looking around the pub to see who was about. Gemma, intrigued, leaned forward and nodded her head.

"Yes of course, what is it" she said.

"Well the woman's files were locked away, only a court order could get to them but then we were told they were lost? Anyway my Solicitor, who is very good and knows a lot of people on both sides of the law, managed to get a copy of her file. Where and how I never asked him and he did it just to get some background on what we were dealing with"

"Really, well please tell all"

"Ok she never knew her mother because she died in childbirth, in that very house. She was brought up by her father, who owned that house. Anyway he abused her from a very early age and raped her daily. She got pregnant on more than one occasion, but he got rid of them"

"Holy fuck" Gemma said taking another drink and listening intensely

"Anyways it seems when she was around seventeen she had a child, the father went missing around this time, his whereabouts or body has never been found. She apparently killed the child, and kidnapped a pregnant girl from the village and tried to take the child from inside her, which went disastrously wrong" he looked around again keeping his voice low.

"And they let this bitch back out on the street?" Gemma gasped.

"She was committed before she left her teens, was in there for over twenty-five years, released and is now on medication to control her mental state" he leaned back and sighed out.

"So they knew what she was, they knew what she had done and they were still trying to fucking defend her? That bastard who interrogated me, I could have smacked him in the bloody mouth I can tell you"

"They do not like their dirty washing done in public, but please tell no one especially Diana what I have told you, it is all confidential and was obtained illegally no doubt"

"No, no of course not, I will tell no one and thank you for your trust in me. So who was that weirdo with the funny eyes?" she said finishing her drink

"It is a bit of a mystery who he was, been hanging around the place for years looks like he was run away who was taken in way back. Village idiot or something, we are not too sure?"

"What a bloody village and area that is, I will be glad never to go back there. Don't worry, I won't tell a soul, it will be our secret" she smiled at him.

"You are a good girl Gemma, thank you, would you like another or is this your lunch hour?"

"Half hour, thank you but I have to get back. We have a client coming in this afternoon, a potential lot of business and boss wants us all there looking nice and busy"

"Oh ok I won't keep you then, but I think I might have one more" he smiled and stood up as Gemma did; they friendly hugged and said goodbye. He went back to the bar and Gemma went outside to her car. The young boy on the bike was sat looking at her from the other side of the car park. His head was tilted down and he was hunched awkwardly on the saddle. One foot resting on the bike's peddle and the other on the ground. Gemma paid him no attention but when she was not looking he took out a mobile phone and clicked a few photos of her. She drove off and he just watched her go. It was about twenty minutes later when Conrad came out. The bike rider was still there and did the same with Conrad, took a photo of him and the car. When he had driven away, the bike rider lifted his head and looked up. It was not a boy after all, it was a small woman. Brown hair cut short and much fatter in the face, obviously had put some weight on. She didn't have any makeup on or anything that would draw attention. No it was not a boy at all, it was Helen. She looked different enough not to be recognised and not a little old lady anymore.

For all intents and purposes, a young teen age boy on a push bike, keeping themselves to themselves. Not bothering anyone and no one bothering him but actually watching and gathering information and hiding in plain sight. Setting off she rode her bike down the road the same way Conrad had gone, the same road she had been going down for weeks now. Familiarising herself with the area. Knowing the roads, the short cuts and knowing the routines of Gemma and Conrad. She knew where they lived, she was beginning to know when they left and came home. She had not seen Diana much, just once when Gemma took her out in the car. She has grown her hair, it was much longer now, a different style when Helen saw it. She turned up her lips in disgust and instantly disliked it. Waiting for her time, Helen rode along the road and had found a place to squat. She had stolen money and robbed unsuspecting people at night. Keeping a low profile during the day she just kept herself to herself and kept any contact with people to a minimum. Biding her time she put together her gathered information and was planning her attack. Not sure when or where yet but she would keep going until something dropped into place. No matter how long it would take she would do it. Relentless, indefatigable she would make sure what she wanted would be done, her revenge for them ruining everything and not complying with her wishes. Riding along the road she shot off to the edge and down a walkway with steel railings on either side. Heading across the waste ground she came up to the hill. Getting off the bike she pushed it and walked by the side of it. Heading up and across the old railway yard and abandoned signal house, she looked around to make sure there was no one about. Then ducking down to the edge and along the bushes, she went thought a gap pulling a bush across as she went through behind the hole. This took her into the old and falling down derelict house that stood on the lines. Obviously not used for years and left to rot, it was boarded up. All the doors and windows had sheet chip board over them and it looked sealed up. She went to the back and pulled the board off the backdoor, she had prised it off a while ago when she found the place.

She went in and pulled the board back into its hole. From the outside nothing looked changed; no one would know that she was there. Leaving the bike by the door, she walked into the dark room. The only light came from the hole in the roof upstairs; she headed up the wooden bare steps and into this room. She had a tent already up and nailed in place on the wooden floor. A small stove with a pan on it and two boxes by the side with various items in them including clothes. The holdall bag she took from the car of the two people who gave her a lift was inside the tent. It was dry and secure. When it rained, it came in through the roof and ceiling but her tent was pitched at the far said away from the hole so she was not bothered about it. She had several candles scattered around the outside of the tent on the floor. The wax had built up and caused a mound where she had used one and put another. She took off the jacket and lay down on the sleeping bag inside the tent. Taking out the phone which she took the photos with earlier she started to look at them. It was Gemma's old phone that Francis had when Helen grabbed her outside her house. She had kept it and went to the library from time to time to charge it up there from the public charging port situated inside. It was easy to get a charging cable for it. She had taken the sim card out and used it now as a camera and to look at all the photos she had found on it. Looking at the ones she had taken today she then flipped through and looked at the previous ones she had taken. She silently looked as she had Conrad getting into his car, then Gemma leaving Diana's house, Gemma leaving work and Conrad outside the pub. She had lots of photos she had taken and also looked at the ones already on there that Gemma had taken; there was a lot of her and Diana, lots of her being silly, some of her with men, some on holiday and some of a Golden Retriever. Helen had looked at them a hundred times and now decided that Gemma would make a better garden for a seed to be planted so she can get her baby back. Now that Travis was gone she would need someone else to plant the seed. She was sure she would find someone, somewhere that was not her immediate objective, that was how to get Gemma and then kill the others.

# CHAPTER TEN

Diana was ready, her first day at work, she was nervous but also excited. Gemma had offered to take her in, but she insisted she would drive herself. She had to start to get her life back. Checking herself in the mirror and admiring her new longer hairstyle, she smiled. It felt good to do so, she had not smiled much but today she smiled and it was a fresh start. Dressed smart in a trouser suit and looking professional, she was satisfied and headed out. Locking her house up securely and double checking that she did. She went to her car and drove off towards her work. It was her first day at work in quite a while, the nerves were strong and the butterflies were in her stomach but the excitement and the want to get back to normal were stronger. She headed off and slowly drove down the road. Slowing down behind a boy on his bike she waited then took a wide berth around him, the boy lifted his hand in a thank you gesture. Little did she know she had just passed Helen, who had been outside her place expecting Gemma to be there, but was now cursing and heading away. Diana drove steady and made sure she was careful and arrived early. She knew who she had to meet there and was happy to see Gemma stood by her car already, waiting in the car park for her. Waving with a smile Diana then parked up and locked her car, checking the doors afterwards to make sure they were locked. Then she walked over to Gemma and they hugged.

"Wow look at my best mate, all sexy and ready to knock them dead" Gemma said with a big grin on her face and looking Diana up and down.

"Shut up, it is alright do you think?" Diana said asking for her honest opinion.

"We tried on every one of your clothes last night and yes this is it, you look gorgeous, if I were a man I would be straight there" she winked her eye and they laughed and walked into work together Gemma with her arm around Diana's shoulders.

Francis was home alone, Conrad had gone to get the food shopping in, there was definitely improvement there but she still had a long way to go. She picked up her phone and sent Diana a text wishing her well in her new job then went and sat down in the living room. She waited for Conrad to come back. She didn't want to go with him but didn't like to be left alone either. Sitting in the living room she watched out the window. A boy on a bike went past and a few moments later he came back again the opposite way, only this time he stopped in the road and looked at her from outside. She didn't take much notice at first then she began to panic at the boy just parked there, looking into the house through the main window. He had a cap on and his head tilted down so she could not see his face. She looked around the room and could feel the panic rising up inside her. Her hands started to shake and she stood up and stared out at him. But a few moments later he set off and was gone off back down the road. She grabbed her phone and rang Conrad, when he answered he was in the supermarket getting the groceries.

"Francis you all right have you forgotten something on the list?" he asked happily.

"No, please hurry home, there is someone hanging about, I do not feel safe" she whimpered.

"Stop worrying, you are locked in, you have the police number, I will be home shortly, please just calm down Francis everything is fine" he said as reassuring as he could.

"Hurry home please" she said.

"I will be there as soon as I can" he hung up the phone and quickened his step, today it would not be a leisurely stroll around. It would be getting what they wanted as fast as he could and get back home, looks like Francis is having a panic attack day. He sighed and started to hurry and rush around looking at his shopping list and getting what they needed for the week, trying not to forget anything along the way.

Diana had fun at her new job, it was nerve-racking at first but everyone made her feel welcomed and she could do the job easily, that made it a bonus and less stressful for her. It was lunch time and

Gemma was waiting for her as she came across the corridor from her work station.

"How is it going, you been promoted yet?" she said with a smile.

"Hey, it's going really good" They hugged and then walked the short distance down the corridor to the steps then down to the small canteen they had on site. It was a modest place with tables and chairs set out randomly across the room, a drinks machine and a counter that sold sandwiches. Gemma showed her how to get on and asked her what she wanted. Just bottled water and a sandwich, she was not too hungry. They both went and sat by the bay window on the far wall looking out across the car park.

"Yeah it's going good. I was shown around this morning, given a little health and safety talk and all that then shown to my work station. I am going to be able to handle the workload I should think, not a lot different from what I was doing before really" she smiled and took a bite of her sandwich.

"Excellent, I told you it would be fine, not the best paying job but you will soon move up, just show them how wonderful and talented you are" Gemma said taking a drink of her water and opening her own sandwich from its cellophane wrapper.

"Well thank you Gemma, I owe you so much, how can I ever repay you?"

"Oh shut up, we are best friends, nothing is done for reward it's done for wine and a Chinese" she laughed and took a bite of her sandwich then her face changed with the taste of it.

"You silly arse, but you got it" Diana said taking another bite.

"This sandwich has died and gone to hell I think, what is it suppose to be?" she said looking at the wrapping she just took off.

"Mine is ok, tastes alright, I got a chicken salad" Diana said taking another bite.

"God knows what I got but it isn't an egg and mayonnaise salad, or if it is then it is from another planet, tastes like shit" she spoke her last few words loud so the staff at the food counter could hear her but she carried on eating it all the same. She then took a long drink of her water and put it back down on the table, stretching her arms up and sighing out.

"You ok, you look tired?" Diana asked.

"I am fine, early night for me tonight I think"

"Oh I am sorry, I did keep you up late I suppose getting your critical opinion on my wardrobe for today?" she smiled and finished her sandwich off, then took a drink of her water.

"Shut up, how about a girl's night in this weekend, wine and Chinese to celebrate your new job, the future is ours girl, what do you say?" she asked eagerly.

"Fuck it, yeah why not, the past is gone, I am not going to live my life in fear of it, let's look forward and to the future, wine and Chinese it is my good friend" Diana said with a big genuine smile. She was feeling happy again and finally being able to control her fear. She would never forget it but at least she could keep it down where it belonged and control it, she had stopped letting it control her.

"Wow, yes, excellent so glad you coming back girl, lets live the life we have to the fullest! The past is gone, just makes you realise how important it is to enjoy your life and the future"

"I second that motion" she took a drink of her bottled water, looking at Gemma who was smiling big with happiness and relief.

"Ok, where are we going on holiday, I want sun, sea, sand, sex and lots of hunky men to drool over" Gemma said quite loudly and the rest of the canteen heard her.

Diana gulped and laughed while she was drinking and spilt it down on top of the table, still giggling then looking up at Gemma who was laughing at her. It all felt good and it all was easing her agony of the last few months. Diana was finally feeling better about herself and the future. She owed so much to her friend and would never forget it. The half hour went very quickly and they were soon were back at work.

Conrad was sat with Francis and they had just finished their lunch. He had filled the dish washer and it was running happily away in the kitchen. Francis held onto him and rested her head on his chest, he put his arm around her and let her settle and snuggle into him.

"I bet you think I am bloody stupid don't you?" Francis said not moving her head from where she was comfortable and felt safe.

"Oh shut up, no I do not think any such thing, you are recovering great, you had a very disturbing and traumatic experience and it is just going to take some time" he told her reassuringly and kissed the top of her head.

"I don't really deserve you do I" she said pulling into him even more.

"Don't talk silly you are all I have ever wanted, we are indestructible you and me. Now Diana is back and returning to us so all is good, be positive and look on the bright side, the future is where we are not going back"

"You are right, I am glad I didn't go onto them tablets, antidepressants like the doctor suggested. It is alright getting on them but it is getting off the bloody things again I have heard. I don't like it and didn't want to do it, you are my antidepressant anyway"

"I don't blame you; I will do my best, all we have is each other and Diana, and that is all that counts in this world. Nothing will ever spoil that again" he pulled his arm in and gave her a squeeze. She loved it and closed her eyes enjoying the feeling of security and love she felt from him. It was the best feeling in the world to her. Closing her eyes she drifted off into a rested sleep and he put his head back and relaxed, closing his eyes too for their afternoon nap.

Gemma was ready to leave bang on the button and raced down to where Diana was supposed to be, but she saw her in the office with her new Boss. She then she looked at her phone and saw a missed text. It was from Diana saying she had to have a meeting with her new boss and would be out a little late, catch you tonight. Gemma sighed and sent one back saying ok. She knew her boss and knew he would have her in there for an hour telling her about the place and how he wants things run, it would be all very boring but they had all been through it.

She went off and headed for the exit out to the car park. Getting into her car she positioned herself and looked at herself in the mirror straightening her hair then started her car. She drove off slowly and out of the car park, reaching down and turning up the CD player she sang along to the old song playing. It was a good clear night and she was looking forward to getting home and taking a shower. She was up all night helping Diana and now she was shattered. She headed into town then out across the back way, it was longer but she avoided a lot of traffic this way. The road was quite narrow in places but she knew it well and driven here many times. Singling along to her song she took it steady. Then out of nowhere a boy on a push bike came from the side and she hit him. She cursed and slammed on her breaks, racing out of the car. The boy was out in front and his bike knocked off to the side; he was getting up when she reached him

"Oh my God, are you alright? Where the hell did you come from?" she said helping him up and was going to reach down to pick his cap up but froze as she did. The knife was large and looked very sharp. It was now touching her throat she looked right into the eyes of Helen.

"Try anything you bitch and you are dead, we are going to walk to the car and you are going to get into the boot slowly do you understand?" Helen barked at her with a lower voice then she had before. Her face was different, fuller and fatter and her hair shorter and now brown. Gemma had no mistake about who this was. Her heart was racing and she felt the grip of fear grab her from deep within once again. They walked to the back of the car and Helen instructed her to open it, she did so and climbed in. Reaching into the side pocket of the jacket she had on, Helen took out an already half pulled bag tie. She looped this around Gemma's feet and pulled it tight. It cut into her and instantly felt uncomfortable. Still holding the knife by her throat she shouted at her,

"Put your hands together and out so I can see them here," when Gemma did what she was told, Helen took a second plastic bag tie and looped this around her hands and pulled it tight across her wrists. She then pushed her back and slammed the boot closed. Gemma was uncomfortable, scared and in total darkness.

Helen got into the driver's seat and looked down seeing Gemma's phone. She picked it up and threw it out of the window then drove away steadily down the road. Putting the knife down by her feet she settled in and had a blank unemotional look on her face and just carried on driving towards her hideout. She arrived shortly after and parked by the locked gate, she looked around and waited until the road was quiet then got out of the car and opened the gate. She had bust the lock and chain off it before she left. She drove through then went and put the lock and chain back on so it looked like it was still secured and not been touched. She drove down the overgrown pathway towards the old derelict house. Parking around the outer side so no one could see the car, she stopped and got out; taking the keys from the car she looked around once again and went to the boot. Opening it she looked in at Gemma still laid there staring up at her and saying nothing.

"You do as you are told and you do not get cut, you make me angry you get this blade deep inside you, do I make myself clear?" Helen asked holding the blade again to her throat.

Gemma nodded and then said "yes", Helen took the knife and cut the ties around her ankles, and then she gestured with the knife for her to get out. Gemma struggled to do it with her hands tied but she managed it. Helen pushed her violently towards the door.

"Take that down slowly" she said pointing at the boarded up doorway. The knife was in Gemma's side and she so wanted to make a move but thought it just a bit too risky with the blade so close so she did as she was told. Taking the board off she was pushed inside and told to sit on the floor which she did. Helen then put the board back to make it look like no one was here. She grabbed Gemma by the hair and pulled her close holding the knife to her eyeball. She smiled and put her face very close to Gemma's and sniffed her.

"I can smell fear and it has a sweet smell you know? Now we are going up those stairs and if you try anything I will fucking cut you up into small pieces and send you to your friend's one bit at a time, do you understand me?" she sounded quite mad and seemed to enjoy what she was saying, and the fear it ignited. Gemma just nodded, she stood up and the knife was brought to her throat again. Helen came around the back of her, she grabbed her hair and pulled her head back exposing her throat and the knife was now resting on it. They carefully and slowly went up the stairs and Helen told her where to go. When they reached the tent Helen pushed her violently down, Gemma fell painfully onto the floor. She noticed that some strong, large hooks had been already screwed deep into the wooden floor boards.

"You sit there and put a leg out so your feet are touching them hooks" Helen ordered and brought some more plastic, strong bag ties out from the tent. She put one around Gemma's ankle and through a hook pulling it tight and secured her to it then she did the same with the other ankle. Gemma was tied and secured tightly to the floor now, helpless and scared.

Helen stepped back and took a look, she could see Gemma was tied up and could not move so for now it would do. She took the jacket off then came up and sat down in front of Gemma, her new prize, her new toy and soon to be new carrier of her baby.

"What the fucking hell do you want, why are you doing this?" Gemma said finally getting her nerve and full senses back after the initial shock of it all.

"You will carry a baby for me, my baby. We are going to my house and you will do as I tell you, not like that other one she was not what I thought she was" Helen said in a matter of fact tone that did not match the situation or what she had just done at all. There was no remorse or empathy there and she could see nothing wrong with what she was doing.

Gemma looked at her face, a face she never wanted to see again and just shook her head; she could see the woman was disillusioned and insane but didn't know how to handle the situation really so just tried her best.

"You can't get away with this, we know who you are and the police know who you are"

"Well I do not care about that, what we are going to do is this, first you are going to get me into their house and then I will kill them, all of them. After that we are going back to my house and you are going to carry my baby. I was brutally raped and beaten so I can't have children anymore, the things they put up inside me would make your skin crawl. Do you know once was because I didn't do what they wanted so they put a bottle all the way up inside me then they kicked me to the floor and carried on kicking me until the bottle broke inside me, and they call me mentally disturbed?"

"Who, who did this to you?" Gemma asked not knowing whether to believe her or not.

"Another time I was being beaten while one masturbated, and when they stopped he complained because he had not cum yet so they carried on until he had finished"

"Who did these things to you?" Gemma again asked her.

"And they call me mentally insane? Another time and place I was tied to a bed and he let men come in and do what they wanted with me, he made money from it. Sick bastards came in and paid to spend an hour with me doing whatever they wanted and no one would ever know, and they call me mentally disturbed?" Helen was talking but there was no emotion or feeling in her words, they just came out of her mouth and she had a blank expression while she was saying them. She stared at the floor and was silent; she stopped talking and seemed to be miles away with her thoughts.

"Listen Helen, listen to me, you do not have to do this, I can see you have been abused and had a terrible life but please, stop. Let me go and I promise I will..." she was not allowed to finish. Helen came over to her and punched her hard in the face, bloodying her nose. The blow was a shock to her system and it knocked her head back painfully. Helen then went back and sat in front of her unaffected and started to run the blade of the knife across the wooden floorboards for a few moments. She then looked up and stared Gemma in the eye and started to talk again.

"When we go back to my house I will show you where some of it happened, and you can stay there until the baby is due, after that you must go, go away"

186

"You do not have a house anymore, it is gone didn't you see it explode and burn down?"

"Liar, I do not like people who lie to me! People have lied to me all my life, ever since I was a little girl people have lied to me. This won't hurt but it did and this is for your own good but it wasn't. I am only doing this because I love you but he didn't" she shook her head and stared down at the knife again as she dug it deep into the wooden floor. Gemma could see she was remembering things and seemed lost within her memories.

"I am not lying it was destroyed, it is not there anymore" Gemma said blowing the blood down her nose so she could breathe easier.

"How long have you been fucking Diana's father? I have seen you with him, secret meetings in the pubs? You are a filthy whore, he is your best friend's dad and old enough to be your father, or do you like it, do you call him daddy?" She didn't look up from the floor when she asked the question but her grip on the knife got tighter.

"No, no I am not, we are just friends that is all" shaking her head Gemma kept trying to squeeze out of the tie around her wrists. She was sure she had seen somewhere how to get out of them and she was trying to remember how to do it. Twisting her wrists was painful then she remembered that you put them above your head and swiftly bring your hand down towards the ground while spreading your hands apart. She had seen it done once on a TV program. Keeping this in mind she then looked at her ankles tied up with them also to the hooks, this was going to be harder and much more difficult.

"Why are you looking at them zip ties?" Helen asked her not looking up from the floor.

"They are very painful and stopping my circulation could you please loosen them"

"You really think I am stupid don't you? You have no idea really because you are so ignorant and live in your safe little world outside and you would not last two minutes inside where I have been"

"You are going to get me into their house and watch me kill them with this knife, taste their blood then we are going to take a trip back to my house and get the seed planted in you so I can have my baby" Helen did not move her head but looked up with her eyes and stared at Gemma for the longest time. It made Gemma very uncomfortable and she didn't know what to say or where to look. Lifting the knife Helen stabbed it into the wooden floor and left it there in front of her so she could see it and then she went into the tent.

Gemma sighed out and tried to work her leg up and down, she was trying to rub the bag tie on the metal hook where it was fastened around. She could get a little movement but not much. She worked it up and down and she was pretty confident she could get it off her wrists but she needed her legs free as well or she was a sitting duck and she knew it. Twisting her feet she started to move it against the metal moving it every way she could, working the plastic against the rougher metal of the hook. She knew she was on limited time and worked fast.

She could hear Helen talking to herself in the tent then she started to shout and argue with herself in a violent voice. She could see her moving about and slapping herself in the tent. It was disturbing to see and hear but it made her work faster to get free of her ties. Suddenly Helen came charging out of the tent screaming and pulling at her own hair. She was shaking her head and grinding her teeth together. She looked enraged and stomped over to where the knife was and pulled it out of the floor. She started to wave it around and stab the air with it then suddenly she stopped and was calm again. She threw the knife down and it stuck back into the wooden floor. She walked over to Gemma and sat crossed legged in front of her. Her eyes were red, bloodshot and she was breathing heavily. Staring at Gemma she didn't move for a while and Gemma didn't know where to look.

"Do I make you nervous?" Helen finally asked.

"You would make anybody nervous" Gemma felt compelled to say.

"You killed Travis; you attacked him in the kitchen."

"No I didn't kill anyone" Gemma shook her head.

"Little Travis came to us, we found him one day crying down by the lake. He had ran away and my dad took him in. He became part of the family, he was my friend and you killed him"

She nodded a yes in disagreement and counter to Gemma's shaking of her head.

"That's not true, we didn't kill him but he was going to kill Diana" Gemma defended.

"Good, that little stupid bitch got on my nerves, thinking I was Aunt Rose. What a pathetic woman Rose was, she was an imposter do you know that, trying to be me, wanted to take over my life and become me but I saw what she was doing and put a stop to it"

"I will put a stop to them all, you are going to get me into their house and I am going to kill them all and then you are going to grow me a baby" Gemma could see Helen was mad. She repeated herself, had no feeling, no conscience and no knowledge of right or wrong. She was highly dangerous and all she could do was humour her to keep her calm.

"I will do anything you want, please could you just loosen the ties, please they are digging very painfully into my ankles" Gemma asked once again.

"Do you know what I did once to someone in one of those places? Shall I tell you? I dug both my thumbs into their eyes, pushed the eyeballs right back into the skull. I felt them pop under my thumbs, pushed them right into their brain" There was no regret, compassion or empathy when she was talking and this is what scared Gemma the most.

"Please, please" Gemma found herself saying, as the panic started to set in and she started to feel helpless and vulnerable. She had to get her feet untied then she would have a chance she thought, she had to try something. She knew she had to at least try something.

"Do you realise how useless that word is? I have said it ten thousand times and no one listens. It is like an invisible word because no one sees it or hears it. It must be a silent word do you think?"

"I, I don't, don't know" Gemma stammered her words out as the fear started to win her over.

"Please, yes it is a useless word. No one takes any fucking notice of it so let us now stop using it, no more is that word to be said. It no longer exists in our vocabulary"

Biting her lip Gemma shifted on the floor she was becoming very uncomfortable and the stress was setting in, not only mentally but physically too. She was in the same awkward position and she didn't like it. Again Helen became quiet, she just stared down at the knife in front of her and then she stood up not saying another word as she went back into the tent.

Taking her chance Gemma lifted her hands high above her head and swiftly brought them down in front of her, pulling her wrists apart as she did. It didn't work and she started to panic as her wrists were still securely tied. She tried again and to her utmost relief she did it, the bag tie broke off her wrists. Her hands were free, she looked over to the tent and then reached out she could just touch the knife. She moved, stretched and managed to get her fingers on the top of the handle then pushed forward and grabbed it pulling it up and out of the floor. She quickly cut the plastic tie on her left ankle then her right. She was free and stood up looking back towards the tent she screamed. Helen was stood there just smiling and looking at her. She slowly rolled up her sleeves to her elbows, interlocking her fingers she stretched her palms out cracking the joints of her fingers then smiling wider at Gemma. She slowly walked out and started to come forward.

"Stay back, I am not joking, you fucking stay there, I have this knife" Gemma shouted holding the knife out in front of her.

"Gemma Dear, have you ever stabbed anyone before? Thrust the blade in and heard the squelching sound and the blood, oh lots of blood especially when you pull the blade out. If you can pull it out of course, the vacuum locks the blade sometimes. You have to twist and move it to let air in, that is why some blades have a groove along the side did you know that?" she was still smiling and walking forward. Gemma was backing up, the knife trembling in her hands as she swallowed and screamed at Helen.

"Fucking stay there, do not come any fucking closer"

"Now now baby no need for all this. I hope you are not going to be this excitable when you carry the baby, it will upset the poor little mite" Helen smiled and stopped in front of Gemma who was staring wide eyed at her and sweating, shaking uncontrollably.

"Stay there, the police will be here, they will" she said.

"Not as easy as it looks is it? Looks simple in the movies doesn't it? Oh I will just stab someone but when you are faced with it, when you have the blade there in your hand can you do it? Can you plunge that blade into this little old ladies guts, spill her blood and intestines all over the floor? Makes a hell of a mess, can you do it Gemma, can you?"

"Shut up just shut up, please" Gemma insisted.

"Invisible word, never heard it. Let me tell you I am going to come for you and you will have to stab me with that knife, not just once but many times. I will not stop coming just because you do it once, unless you cut my throat that is. Think you can stab me in the throat? Now that is a lot of blood, a main artery, the heart just pumps it out, literally. Makes a hell of a mess, I know I have done it" she tilted her head and smiled at her again. She seemed to be enjoying what she was doing and watching Gemma shake and sweat.

My phone would have been tracked by Diana, we had a lock on each other's phone so by now the police will be on their way" Gemma told her looking behind her for a moment to see where she could back up to if she had to keep going.

"Wow that is clever isn't it but your phone is out there somewhere and we are in here" Helen laughed and started to giggle. She was actually enjoying watching Gemma squirm and shake in front of her. Gemma was surprised just how hard this was, she thought she would be able to just pick up the knife, be in charge and not have to use it. But here and now confronted with the choice, she was not sure she could do it and not sure it she had the nerve.

"I will tell you what I am going to do, just this once because I am feeling generous. You put that knife down and I will not gouge your fucking eyes out with a spoon and feed them to you, because you see you do not need eyes to give me my baby"

194

Just then in the distance they could hear police sirens, they were a bit away but approaching fast. Helen frowned and looked a little confused. She looked in the direction of the noise then back at Gemma who on hearing them suddenly got some courage and much needed nerve.

"GPS on my car you daft bitch, track my phone and my car. You are fucking finished!" Gemma breathed in and suddenly felt more in control knowing help was on the way. Helen stared at her and smiled again, she seemed unaffected.

"Maybe but the question still remains can you use that knife, can you kill? Once you have you are never the same again, never the same person. So they catch me so what, I am crazy, they will send me back to a hospital. I know how to beat the system and tell them what they want to hear. What you fail to understand is they don't want people like me in those places and they don't want those places anymore. Probably Broadmore, that is the big famous one isn't it? The one place I have not been to yet" she smiled again completely unconcerned the sirens were getting louder and as they did Gemma was getting braver.

"I will make sure you are fucking locked up and never get out, sick fucks like you deserve to go to the electric chair"

"England never used the electric chair; we used hanging, the last of which was in 1964 and capital punishment abolished in

1969. So you see you do not know what the hell you are talking about do you" Helen took a big intake of breath then sighed out. She stopped smiling and looked at Gemma right in the eyes; her own eyes were cold, heartless and had no emotion whatsoever behind them. Dead eyes and Gemma got a cold shiver down her spine.

The police were racing down the road as they had a lock on Gemma's car and were only minutes away from its location. Diana was in the back of one of the cars and sat with a police woman. She had insisted on coming along and was only there because they may needed to use her to mind game with Helen if the opportunity arose in some way. They had a psychiatrist in route and were almost at the location themselves.

"Times up, let's see what Gemma is made of" then without warning she shrieked at the top of her voice and raced forward in a dash towards Gemma who panicked and backed up but could not go any further. She slashed the blade out and caught Helen across the chest but she didn't stop. Helen punched and scratched at Gemma's face and wrestled onto the floor fighting for the knife. Although Helen was much older and smaller, Gemma was surprised how strong and vicious she was. She could not keep her off and just kept a tight grip of the knife. Fighting on the floor they scrambled about. The police burst through the gate and raced to the

196

derelict house. They spotted the car and two officers got out and searched around for a way in. The police woman in the back held onto Diana and told her to stay in the car. A second police car came screeching down and stopped a little behind the first one, two more officers got out and one ran around the back and the other went to join the first two. Diana saw one of the first officer's prise the wood off which was over the doorway. He pulled it off and cautiously looked inside. Then they shouted Gemma's name. They dashed in quickly when she shouted for help from upstairs. Helen was punching Gemma relentlessly in the face and was now holding the knife; she brought it up and was going to stab it down into Gemma's blood splattered face but a strong arm pulled her back. The two police officers were they just in the nick of time to save her. One officer helped to get Gemma up and away safely, the other fought with Helen who was fighting like a wild cat. The officer had no choice but to swing her and violently throw her off to the side. She still had the knife and rolled awkwardly away when she landed. The officer took out a taser gun and pointed it at Helen as she stood up spitting and grinding her teeth, mumbling some obscenities at him.

"You stop there, do not move, put the knife down" the police officer commanded. The second officer took his Extendable ASP baton out and flicked it out to its full extent in one hand and had his

CS spray in the other. Both officers confronted her and she then suddenly became calm and just smiled.

"Put the knife down, slowly on to the floor" the officer said holding the taser gun on her. Helen just smiled and looked across at Gemma, she kept looking at her in the eye then she lifted her hands and suddenly jabbed the knife into her own neck. Not taking her eyes off Gemma, she pulled it across the inside of her throat and pulled it out severing her own windpipe from the inside out. The blood was gushing out and the police officers ran forward to see what they could do. The third officer had dashed up and was instantly on his radio calling for an ambulance. Gemma started to sob, she was shaking and the third officer came and took her out while his two colleagues tried in vain to stop the bleeding and save Helen. Gemma was greeted by Diana and they hugged and cried together. The police woman sat them in the back of the car. They knew now it was over, they knew now they could really make a fresh start, they knew now the threat and evil was gone. It was a time to heal and to get their lives back together. None of them would ever be the same again but while they had each other they would get through it and get their lives back. Nothing would ever come between them, their bond was strong before but now it was invincible and unbreakable.

The following year the wildlife returned to the lake, the trees bloomed around it and the birds sang again. It was as if they knew, something had gone and the lake could breathe once more after holding its breath for so long. The water became clearer, fresher and the fish returned somehow. It was strange but it was there, the lake lived once again.

The house was gone, the lake's life was back and the stagnant atmosphere seemed to be lifted. No one talked about it, no one wanted to remember but no one could explain it either. It all fell into a hidden, forgotten history. The people who experienced it would never tell and would not want to ever relive it. After years when people visited there, maybe just passing through they would comment how lovely and tranquil it was, how peaceful and picturesque. Not knowing and never knowing what happened here. What secrets the lake held for all those years, but has now given up and is free once again.


The End

OTHER TITLES FROM THE SAME AUTHOR

THE PARA
VENTRILOQUIST
BROKEN
HIDDEN DARKNESS
BROTHERHOOD THE PARA 2
SECOND CHANCE
LUGHOLE AND THE YORKSHIRE MICE

.

Printed in Great Britain
by Amazon

37467394R00118